# Hot Latin Docs

*Sultry, sexy bachelor brothers on the loose!*

Santiago, Alejandro, Rafael
and Dante Valentino are Miami's most
eligible doctors. Yet the brothers' dazzling
lives hide a darker truth—one which made
these determined bachelors close their
hearts to love years ago…

But now four feisty women are about to
turn the heat up for these sexy Latin docs
and tempt them each to do something they
never imagined…get down on one knee!

Find out what happens in:

*Santiago's Convenient Fiancée*
by Annie O'Neil

*Alejandro's Sexy Secret*
by Amy Ruttan

*Rafael's One Night Bombshell*
by Tina Beckett

*Dante's Shock Proposal*
by Amalie Berlin

All available now!

Dear Reader,

Have you ever loved a series—book/film—so much that you couldn't wait to talk about the latest instalment with someone else who loved it too?

Brainstorming and writing the Hot Latin Docs quartet with Annie O'Neil, Amy Ruttan and Tina Beckett was like that for me! When an email pinged on our email loop, my excitement demanded I stop *everything* and go and bask in the latest awesome idea, or devour a snippet one of the other authors had shared from their work in progress.

Dante's not an easy man to love. Halfway through writing this book even *I* became afraid he couldn't be saved. Thank you, Amy Ruttan, for talking me down! So I pushed on through, and now I know: it takes a strong heroine to save a broken man hidden behind his gorgeous smoke and mirrors.

All my characters become real to me as I write their stories, but these lovely ladies have made Dante's whole family real to me now too.

Thank you for picking up *Dante's Shock Proposal*, and if this is your first Hot Latin Doc please search out *Santiago's Convenient Fiancée*, *Alejandro's Sexy Secret* and *Rafael's One Night Bombshell*.

Happy reading!

*Amalie* xo

AmalieBerlin.com/Contact

Facebook.com/AuthorAmalie

# DANTE'S SHOCK PROPOSAL

BY
AMALIE BERLIN

MILLS &
BOON®

First published in Great Britain 2017
By Mills & Boon, an imprint of HarperCollins*Publishers*
1 London Bridge Street, London, SE1 9GF

Large Print edition 2017

© 2017 Amalie Berlin

**LP**

ISBN: 978-0-263-06716-3

**Amalie Berlin** lives with her family and critters in Southern Ohio, and writes quirky and independent characters for Mills & Boon Medical Romance. She likes to buck expectations with unusual settings and situations, and believes humour can be used powerfully to illuminate truth—especially when juxtaposed against intense emotions. Love is stronger and more satisfying when your partner can make you laugh through times when you don't have the luxury of tears.

Visit the Author Profile page
at millsandboon.co.uk for more titles.

To Amy, Annie, and Tina.
Expect me to whine incessantly until we do this
again! No, really. When *are* we going to do this
again? How does *now* work for y'all?

Amy: will pretty much always be jealous of
your inspirational idea—Magic Mike: surgeon.
Thank you for your tireless friendship,
and for seriously raising the bar! *luff*

Annie: for being an amazing, energetic weirdo
who makes this hyperactive purple-haired lunatic
feel right at home! And being the other *quirky*
medical writer. ☺ Ugly Sisters 4 Evah!

Tina: this marks our third author-led collaboration
and it keeps getting better! Thank you for
continuing to come back and try again. ♥

Laura McCallen: sorry for being such a pain!
And thank you for not only whipping the proposal
into shape, but for all you've done to work with
me—this year's been a tricksy one! ♥

### Praise for
### Amalie Berlin

'Amalie Berlin has proved she's one of the
best medical authors of today, and her stories
will for ever have a place on my reading shelf!'
—*Contemporary Romance Reviews* on
*Return of Dr Irresistible*

# CHAPTER ONE

SHE WAS BEING stood up.

Badgered into a blind date by her coworkers, and they hadn't even picked a responsible man who'd actually show up to the club where he'd asked her to meet him.

Nurse Lise Bradshaw looked at her watch for the tenth time in twenty minutes, waved down a server, ordered a mojito, then let herself look somewhere besides the door she'd been staring at since arriving.

*Don't think about him.*

*Don't think about any of it.*

To heck with judgmental people who had no idea what it was like to date in the current decade and absolutely didn't support her life plan.

No one here knew she'd been stood up, and even if they figured it out, she didn't know any of them anyway.

The music was good. Tonight could be an embarrassing footnote to her week, or it could be the fun she'd dressed for. Even if she was there alone, no one was ever really alone on a dance floor in South Beach.

If, by some miracle, her date managed to drag his sorry butt to the club, amid the black and white decor, her slinky red wrap dress would stand out whether it was crowded or not, and it was still too early to be hopping.

In her safe, quiet life, Lise went to work, worked hard, read a lot, and planned for her future—a future where she'd have a family again. She didn't go clubbing with her coworkers, and had no close friends to speak of since moving from Jacksonville to Miami—so didn't go dancing with them either. Basically, she didn't go clubbing. If—no, when—she managed to get her plan rolling, there wouldn't be any nights in her future for dancing, so she might as well make the most of it.

She'd agreed to the fix-ups not because she ever wanted to replicate her parents' deadly marriage but because she wanted to fully enjoy her remaining not-pregnant weeks.

Her mojito arrived and she downed half of it before helping herself to the dance floor.

Instruments sat ready on a stage elevated at the far side of the dance floor, promising live music later. But for now the DJ's choice got her feet and body moving, and they could put the song on repeat for the whole evening for all Lise cared.

Staking out a corner near the stage, she closed her eyes and let the music take her. Most of the lyrics shot past her, but she picked up on enough to get the meaning. The beat filled in the rest, and she let it wash away the week's frustration and worry, let it warm her belly...or maybe that was the mojito.

Three songs in, the music faded, but another song didn't start. She stopped her swinging beat and opened her eyes, her gaze landing on musicians striding past her to the stage.

A tall man in a three-piece black suit and shirt—jacket missing—and a black fedora pulled low met her gaze as he walked past her.

Eyes black as his suit connected with hers, and Lise felt the thrill of shared attraction before recognition seared through her.

Those eyes. She knew those eyes. Her breath stuttered, heat flaring in cheeks and racing down over her neck and chest.

*Dr. Valentino.*

While not technically her boss, she worked too closely at his side in surgery with masks covering everything but those eyes for her not to recognize them.

She would have even if she hadn't also been ignoring an unwelcome lusty crush on the good doctor for the past two years. He looked at her like he wanted to sweep her into his arms and learn her curves right there on the dance floor, like a sugar addict at an all-you-can-eat ice-cream bar. Tempted, with intentions forming...

He'd never looked at her like that before, and she'd always tried hard not to look at him like that.

For all their time working together, she knew next to nothing about him. Great surgeon, freakishly sexy, sometimes testy, and she knew which instruments and techniques he preferred.

Some voice in the back of her mind shook her out of her staring. *Go back to your table, dummy.*

Her feet stayed stuck, like her eyes.

Dr. Valentino headed for a piano at her end of the stage. As he stepped over the bench his gaze connected with hers again, and her stomach bottomed out.

That was desire. Real desire. An honest-to-God, I-want-you-hot-on-this-piano heat, those gorgeous eyes filled with dirty, dirty promises.

How did he do that?

Had he always felt that way but been too proper to show it at the hospital? He could obviously hide things—like musical ability. Like him being in a band and wearing real, non-scrub-like clothing better than anyone had a right to. Who wore a three-piece suit to a nightclub—assuming there was a jacket somewhere around the establishment?

A rush left her feeling powerful and sexy, something she'd not felt in a long time. This was the emotional payoff for the red dress, which had been giving her courage and confidence all evening.

Her date may have stood her up, but she barely gave him a passing thought when Dr. Valentino looked at her like that!

Suddenly his brows snapped down over narrowing dark eyes. A scowl darkened them further and thinned his usually fine mouth. His storm shutters came down hard as he sat at the piano.

First desire—let's have naked fun with this marshmallow fluff kind of dirty, playful sexiness. Then...

It took her a second to riddle it out, and the tipsy alcoholic butterflies in her belly figured it out first, and a ripple of something wrong stole her breath for an entirely different reason.

He hadn't recognized her until he'd sat.

She'd probably been looking at him exactly like she'd been striving not to for two years—suggestively goofy, with added appreciation of his dirty looks. But he'd only just recognized her.

The man never said much outside of delivering orders or maybe some narration for the surgery recordings, so she'd learned to read his eyes, often the only part of his face she could see.

If she'd seen that look over a patient, she'd be readying for the worst.

Her alcoholic butterflies definitely needed another mojito. If the laws of physics could at least be counted on—as it seemed possible they could have suddenly turned against her too—going back to her table to get another glass of liquid forgetfulness would move her far enough outside the glow of spotlights for him to see her. Or how the color of her face currently probably rivaled that of her dress.

Lise unslung the small purse from across her torso, fished out her phone, and set it on the table as the music began. Soon she had another mojito in hand, and having things to fiddle with helped her settle in to listen without worrying about what his scowl had meant.

The music that had been playing before the band had taken to the stage had been modern, Latin pop—mostly Spanish and some Spanglish songs. But the band played something different, and it took her a moment to classify the bright, fevered jazz that rolled off the stage and through the speakers.

It helped a little, though, the idea of leaving tempted. If she ran away, she could have three whole days for him to forget before the usual Monday morning surgery.

But Jefferson might still show up. There existed a slim chance that he'd gotten stuck in traffic or forgotten what time they were going to meet. A terrible accident could excuse not phoning or texting to bow out. If she left now, knowing her luck today, he'd show up and she'd have to reschedule rather than just getting to mark this third date officially off her to-do list without further delaying her life plans.

The band had either practiced daily or had been playing together for years. The arrangements gave all instruments and stylings a chance to shine, and no matter the major personality trait Dr. Valentino displayed in every other interaction she'd had with him, he didn't try to dominate the music like he took over everything else.

That awful scowl left him before the first song finished. Tension flowed off him, brows and posture relaxed. He enjoyed it, clearly, and was good.

By the time the set finished just over an hour later, she'd almost convinced herself that he'd only scowled because he'd given her *The Look*, and she was a coworker. That was all it could be, she hadn't done anything to earn his ire. Could he look at her with unhidden interest then hold it against her because she'd shared it?

Nah… It was consternation over a case of mistaken identity.

But if she trafficked in lies, now would be the time to claim to not have recognized him. The fact that she even considered lying showed how far away from him and his sexy looks she should stay. Lying was a slippery slope. Lies that started out hard to tell became easier, became reflexive… This was just the power of a sexy dress and mojitos mixed with her lusty crush. It made her react uncharacteristically, and she'd own it.

If it came up.

She would not become her parents.

As soon as the lights lowered at the end of the

set, his gaze found her again and she did the only thing she could think to do: lift her now-empty glass in a socially ludicrous toast.

He stood, no sign of the scowl, hopped down from the stage, and made a beeline directly for her.

"Another drink, Bradshaw?"

*Last names. Yes. Good. Like at work.*

"I wasn't asking but, sure, if you like. I was just apparently trying to wave or toast you with an empty glass because I wasn't paying proper attention, Dr.—"

"Dante." He cut her off as he sat, gesturing to the server, to her, and then back to himself. Two mojitos ordered, he focused on her. "When I'm here, it's Dante."

"Dante…" she repeated, but her tongue felt woolly and unequal to the task of calling him anything other than what she always called him. Having his first name in her mouth felt dangerous, like she could break all her rules. "Thank you, Dante, for the mojito."

Dante inclined his head. "It's just a drink," he said. It was in him to say more, but he had time, and her phone started to buzz. Instantly, he picked it up and checked what was incoming. Text. Jefferson.

Dante knew he tended toward suspicion—he'd learned young that suspicion kept him sharp and alert—and sometimes that alertness was the only thing going for him. If her being there was what it looked like, he just didn't want to have to handle it. Who knew where he'd find another place to relax in peace if his connection with The Inferno was discovered?

"Do you usually answer other people's phones?" she asked, a hint of irritation in her voice and a billboard of irritation on her eyes. As she spoke, she leaned toward him across the small round table, making it hard not to look down that amazing cleavage.

"When they show up at my club, unannounced, on a night I'm playing. Did you take pictures?" Not recognizing the name Jefferson, he didn't immediately open the message, but he did pull his eyes back to the screen and flipped to photos.

Focus on the facts, not the astoundingly luscious body she'd kept hidden in baggy scrubs.

"*Your* club?" she asked, then his questions seemed to sink in and the confused look morphed into a scowl, shadowing her incredibly pretty features. "No, I certainly didn't take any photos of you."

The words out, she snapped her fingers and held out her palm for the phone, the jerky arm movements making her jiggle in her well-filled dress.

Which he would ignore.

Stick with the plan. Handle this. If it was something innocent, he could entertain entertaining her after.

The photos tab contained lots of sunset skies and ocean, along with progress photos on a yellow-painted duck-themed nursery.

*Huh.*

But no pictures of him or the club. "Call or text anyone to say you'd found me here?"

"Why would I do that? Are you in the witness protection program or something? Just give me my phone, Dante." Her frustration…or her drinks…made her practically sing his name, but in a manner he'd not heard since high school. Annoyed. A bit too pointed. Sarcastic.

He ignored it, but had to remind himself who he was speaking to—the best surgical nurse he'd ever worked with. Not someone usually prone to… well, any displays of emotion.

"I don't like my professional and personal lives

to cross. No one knows about The Inferno, and I plan to keep it that way. If it's truly coincidental that you're here, you don't need to speak of it with anyone at Buena Vista."

"Don't tell anyone you're in a boy band. Got it."

Boy band. He laughed despite his intention to intimidate her into following through with his demands. Bradshaw always seemed so calm and professional at work—this smart-mouthed and angry version really shouldn't tickle him.

"You know I don't sit around waiting to gossip about you anyway."

Her squinting eyes got nowhere close to convincing him. How many drinks had she had?

The message. If she was reporting to someone…

He lifted the phone again and read the message. "Who's Jefferson?"

Lise, I've heard many good things about you, and that was the reason I initially agreed to our date. But I've had second thoughts. It seems unfair to lead you on when I've just never been into Large Women.

Unknown name, frankly horrible message—she was telling him the truth. It was only coincidental that she'd happened to come into his club.

"He's no one important," she said, but held her hand out for her phone again. Something stabbed him in the gut—he'd say it was guilt, but, with the things he'd done in the past, only one thing had the power to shame him. No, more like vicarious embarrassment. He hit the back arrow to clear the message from the screen and placed the phone in her upward-turned palm.

"You know, you only ever have to ask me for anything *once*."

If that. She was his favorite surgical nurse for good reason. He scheduled his most difficult surgeries on Mondays and Thursdays—the days he'd been able to claim her from the surgery rotation. He'd even once bribed another surgeon to get her on a Tuesday.

Even without medical school, he wouldn't be surprised to hear of her conducting surgery on the side. With her in the OR, it was almost like having a second surgeon on standby. She anticipated his needs.

It was hard to think of this sexy, sarcastic creature as the same person. Even when she got quiet and the embarrassment he'd known was coming wiped the sass right off her face.

"He stood you up?" Dante asked, more gently than anything else he'd said to her.

"He was supposed to be here an hour ago, but it seems he magnanimously bowed out after leaving me to wait for over an hour, so I didn't meet him and fall helplessly in love...because he's never been attracted to Large Women. Capital L on that."

Like he hadn't read it already.

Large with a capital L. Yeah, that had to hurt.

The mojitos arrived and she took a deep drink. He followed suit, for once not sure what to say. Stood up by someone she'd never met, and she'd worn that dress? That'd have made an impression on the man.

She hit the drink hard and eyed the dance floor again. "They make great mojitos..."

Uncomfortable. Speaking to fill the air with words, any words.

"I always hire good people." He tried again. "Why were you meeting a man you didn't know wearing that dress?"

"You haven't heard the rumor mill?" She leaned forward, elbows on the table, to speak closer. "I'm surprised. Someone questions or lectures me about it nearly every day now."

"I don't chat at work, makes it easier to keep things clean." Which was supposed to make it easier to keep his two worlds separate and ignorant of one another. "So what's the rumor?"

"I'm being fixed up on five blind dates by the more insistent nurses on Eight Blue." The neurological unit at Buena Vista. Their unit. "None of them have been all that thrilling, though. The first two couldn't carry on a conversation if their lives depended on it. Then that jerk, and, you know, I don't care if he didn't show up, he counts as number three. They get two more fix-ups, not three. Not my fault they picked so poorly."

"Why have they focused their attention on you?"

The question she'd been dreading—it had started to feel like a trap anytime anyone asked it—but Lise liked to live her life in the open, so she'd answer. She didn't hide things. She didn't keep secrets. She didn't lie. If someone called a woman Large, Lise would've at least made commentary on people being rude. Unlike Dante.

Whatever. She couldn't waste time working out what was going on in his head. Better to be open, and let the chips fall where they may. It was preferable that people reject her for who she really was than to be fooled into loving her then turn her life inside out when they found out she wasn't perfect.

"Because I decided to start a family on my own, and they're all basically horrified that I'm sperm-shopping or, as they call it, 'giving up on love' and 'not waiting for my soul mate.'" She rolled her eyes, and looked back at the dance floor.

Chatting with Real Living Dante was much less satisfying than sharing the sexy imaginary banter that occasionally took place in her head when she wasn't busy doing something important. Imaginary Dante would've already convinced her that she was perfectly shaped and that he loved the way she looked. Imaginary Dante would've compared her to Venus, and Venus would've come in second.

Imaginary Dante was definitely better.

"I see." He said it like he agreed, pulling her gaze back to him, and there was a look—not *The Look,* a judgmental look. "That's why you have yellow duck nursery photos in your phone?"

"Maybe…"

"Sounds like you're having a bad evening, Bradshaw." He leaned his elbows on the table, like they were close friends who talked close. Definitely not like he was about to kiss her, that'd have been an Imaginary Dante move.

So she leaned back again. "Lise. If I'm calling you Dante, call me Lise."

First he failed to discount the notion that she was overweight, and now dissing her Maternity Manifesto and the awesome, adorable, happy and cheerful ducky room?

*Enough.*

She didn't have to sit with him, pretending not to be bothered by Jefferson's abject failure to arrive, followed up by his text-based slap in the face. This wasn't the hospital, it was a dance club. Dr. Valentino wasn't even there. He was probably off being cold and indifferent while heroically and brilliantly saving lives somewhere, and she didn't like Dante, dance club owner, bar band pianist.

"This night's getting less thrilling by the minute. If you're going to try and speed up the evening's deterioration by lecturing me too, you can…you can just shut it! Because you're rude, and I was going to tell you how wonderful the music was too. But now I'm not going to!"

Because her good friend mojito said it didn't count if you said it like that.

"And, for the record…" she lifted a finger when

he opened his mouth to speak, shouting over the music from across the small table "...if a woman says someone called her Large, Big, or even *Rotund*, and she's not, you're supposed to say that other person is delusional. And even if she is, you have to say something about the other person being rude. That you did neither means you think I'm a Large Woman too, with *all* the capitals. I'm not. So...good day, Dante."

Another song popped onto the house system, perfectly timed. Lise grabbed her purse, slung it back across her torso to leave her hands free for Mr. Mojito, and stepped past him toward the dance floor.

She'd gotten only one foot onto the polished tile floor when a large, warm hand clamped around her free wrist, stopping her escape.

"You're not a Large Woman, Lise. But you do a good job of hiding in oversized scrubs at work." She didn't look back at him, but he spoke the words over her shoulder, so near her ear that goose bumps raced up her arm, away from that warm, talented hand.

Even if he was taking up for Sandy. Sandy, the one who'd picked Jefferson. Sandy, who must've been the one to label her *Large*.

"They're scrubs. And, if you haven't noticed, I'm just a little top-heavy." She turned to face him, and he took the opportunity to catch her mojito before she sloshed the contents on one or both of them, then tilted it back to drain the rest of the minty liquid before dropping the tumbler onto the tray of a passing server.

The man had drunk her mojito. What did someone even say when their mojito was stolen from their own hand?

Keep talking. Being speechless only proclaimed, *I'm out of my depth and not smart enough to keep up with this insane conversation.*

Anything that would keep her from staring at his mouth, and thinking about the kind of lusty crush fantasies that mouth definitely could fulfill if he were so inclined.

Pathetically adolescent and showing how badly she wanted company—enough to go on blind dates. Enough for drinking-glass-inspired lust. Pathetic.

Just. Say. Something.

"These stupid things affect what sizes I can wear, but the scrub tops are standard design, and everyone—even people who are actually proportionally built—looks dumb in them. Except you,

you look good in scrubs for some reason. I'd say you sold your soul for it but we're both already in The Inferno. Besides, they're comfortable, so it's easy to work in them. And if I ever got tops fitting my hip dimensions I'd suffocate in my own cleavage."

*Great. Great visual, strangled by bosoms.*

Dante grinned down at her, her second brush with amusement in his eyes, twice in fifteen minutes.

She still couldn't tell if he was laughing with her, or at her.

Before she could say anything else to embarrass herself, he slipped his arm around her waist and took her newly mojito-free hand, flawlessly maneuvering her into dancing position and steering her backward onto the dance floor.

Breathless, and more than a little gobsmacked, Lise allowed herself to be led. "We're dancing now? Arguing makes you feel like dancing?"

Maybe it was good he'd drunk her mojito, she'd clearly had too many.

The firm arm around her waist pulled her close enough to demonstrate the need for her admittedly tent-like scrub tops—her lower half didn't touch his, but her breasts pressed against the heat of his chest, and her still-free arm went automatically around his shoulders.

"That dress is spectacular, and it fits you very well," He said, hand firm on her waist to turn her into some dance her feet didn't know. "Follow me." He slowed down, stepped back enough for her to see his feet, and after she'd mimicked the pattern a couple times, his firm hands were on her again and he steered her in slow steps around the edge of the now much more crowded dance floor.

Why was she going along with this? She'd gone to the dance floor to get away from him. And because she wanted to dance.

But even with that rude phone business, the man was still incredibly sexy, and she'd been stood up. Dante was a satisfactory stand-in for sure.

*Don't overthink it. Just dance with him.*

"Why this dress when you don't know Jefferson?" he asked again, like she hadn't heard him before and had chosen to answer the other, more important part of his question.

Trying to understand him over the loud music meant she had to stare at his mouth, the corner of which had quirked up.

Everything about this felt out of line.

Stare at his mouth to understand and sound sane. Solid plan.

Pretend to dance like she *wasn't* the offspring of an ostrich and a three-legged goat.

Ignore the tide-like sensations rushing up her arms and over her body from having his hands on her.

No problem.

"I did. And it's new," she admitted, and, as she'd done, he focused his attention on her mouth as she spoke. "I've been thinking of these dates as a kind of last hurrah before motherhood. Because I never really go out. Or date—mostly because it's just way too much trouble. But I thought maybe if Jefferson played his cards right and wasn't..."

"Ugly?"

Lise winced, but nodded.

She should definitely stop talking. If she talked, the truth would come out. If she just didn't say anything, that wasn't lying, even if it was a slippery-slope sort of deception.

Also, she should stop licking her lips.

No matter that recognizing her before had put a damper on his wolfish expression, Dante seemed to have changed his mind. He looked at her mouth longer than she spoke, but his brows had come down in a completely different fashion, sex-laced anticipation darkening his eyes.

She felt her ankle wobble and released his hand to throw both arms around his shoulders, holding tighter to him. The wobbly ankle added one more thing for her to concentrate on than her frazzled brain could handle.

If she wanted—and if she could rationalize hooking up with him in any way that could be considered safe or sane—Dante would be her last hurrah.

A last hurrah of epic proportions. He might even come with mojitos.

Dante didn't say anything, he just pulled her a little closer so that his mouth was at her ear and she could feel the slight stubble on his cheek as he sang the Spanish lyrics softly along with the music.

The shivers his song brought rushing forth across her skin made his arms pull tighter, though he leaned back enough to look into her eyes again.

"You should let me take a picture of you then text it back to him. Make him suffer for his bad decision."

And he wanted her, too. This was actually happening. Dr. Dante Valentino wanted her, even after he'd worked out who she was. Two years of nothing but business between them at the hospital, then they meet once outside the hospital...

Why was he still talking about Jefferson?

"You think that'll make him suffer? For all we know, he snuck in, got one look at me, and left in a hurry."

"He didn't," Dante said, still holding her close, though he'd stopped steering her around and they now swayed in one place at the edge of the stage, out of the way.

"You don't know that."

"I do. He's straight, and if he'd seen you tonight... Trust me."

Trust him. As if that were the easiest thing in the world. Trust the sexy man who led a double life.

On the other hand, what harm could a picture do? Maybe Jefferson wouldn't suffer, but he might feel slightly guilty to see that she'd gotten dressed up and waited for him in a nightclub by herself for so long before he actually called it off. Teach him a lesson for the next woman he got fixed up with.

"Okay," Lise said, pulling back to get her phone from her bag. "But make me look good. Maybe there's some kind of sexy filter we can use."

While she pulled the purse off and hung it properly on her shoulder, he stepped back in to murmur something unbearably sexy in her ear. Warm. Playful. And entirely too Spanish for her to understand at all.

Even after three years in Miami, all she'd managed to understand was *querida*.

But it was enough.

A moment later he'd had her posed under the lights and taken a snap. Before she could even see it, he'd sent the picture to Jefferson.

"What did you say?"

"Nothing."

He handed the phone back. "It's better to say nothing. Then all he'll have is a bunch of questions, and that will make him suffer worse."

She righted her bag and stashed her phone, then found herself back in his arms as a faster song started.

He pulled in close, that sexy mouth and fantastically gravelly voice still singing by her ear. Pressure at her side had her spinning and he stepped in until she felt him against her back, his hands landing on her hips.

This couldn't be the same man.

She looked over her shoulder and saw Dr. Val-

entino, but in nearly every respect he was someone else with only tiny flashes of the man she
knew peeking through—like when he did whatever he wanted and expected people to keep up
or catch up.

Catch up was all she could attempt. "Is this a
salsa?"

"No." His voice came warm at her ear. "It's a
bachata. Simple moves. Hips, feet. Easier. Step-
step-step-tap. Exaggerate the hips with the steps."

Seduced by dancing. That's what this was.
She could spot the symptoms, name them, and
couldn't bring herself to give a damn.

Strong hands on her hips led her through the
steps, the pressure of him at her back steering her
as sure as he'd done when facing her, but in this
position she could get a lot closer—feel the heated
length of him. His thighs brushed the backs of
hers, his chest moved against her back. And her
bottom…

When her body seemed to have learned the
dance, he spun her back to face him and said nothing at all, though the looks he gave her brought
back that surge of bold, powerful sexiness she felt.

Heady and fueled by mojitos and bad decision-
making, Lise stepped in before the dance was

over—breaking step—and leaned up to press her lips to the corner of his mouth. Even side on, he stopped dancing.

He stopped everything.

And he didn't kiss her back.

# CHAPTER TWO

MISTAKE?

Mistake!

Lise broke her half-brave half-kiss and stepped back so swiftly that Dante's arms broke loose from her waist.

"I'm sorry." She touched her mouth, remembered her lipstick, looked at his mouth, and then reached up to start smudging it off as best she could. "That was bad of me. I mean, five minutes ago we were fighting."

Rubbing someone's mouth was almost as personal as kissing them.

Right.

She snatched her hand back. "Really, I'm sorry. I'm going to…"

*Die.*

She pointed back at the table and gave up saying words. A pivot and she hurried off in that direction.

"Stop! Why are you so jumpy?" He caught up

to her in two strides and slung an arm around her waist again, then took the closest hand as well. "You have nothing to apologize for."

"You didn't kiss me back."

"They were signaling me from the stage. Snuck past while we were dancing. There's nothing I'd like to do more than dance with you and kiss the jumpiness out of you. Don't apologize for anything but your aim."

They'd reached the table and he turned her into the chair and scooted it in for her. But when she thought he was going to leave, she felt his hand fist in the back of her hair, heat and awareness spiked her chest. He tugged her head backwards over the chair, arching her neck until she looked straight up at him, the action so sudden, so unexpected, and her rum buzz left her speechless. All she could do was stare up at him. She could feel the pulse in her throat, fast and hard, ever increasing as she watched his expression.

Tight enough to control her movements, but not so tight as to hurt, the tension spreading out over her scalp sent shivers through her.

Swiftly, and with far better aim, he leaned in and covered her mouth with his own.

Lise had never been kissed so thoroughly, so

hungrily. So…shockingly. She felt a kind of limpness creep up her spine and straight to her jaw. His tongue plunged into her mouth, from zero to light speed in seconds, coaxing her to stroke against his.

As if she could even consider breaking away from him in that position, his free hand cupping and holding the front of her throat, fingers stroking there without pressure but still burning her skin. It excited her, coiling in her chest so that she couldn't catch her breath from Dante's brand of blatant sensuality, fueled with more than a hint of danger. The taste of his mouth, a hint of the mojitos they'd been drinking, and something more thrilling than she could even have imagined before that second, intoxicated more fully than alcohol could, and she lost awareness of how long they kissed, knew only that her hands crept up, aching, empty and seeking.

When someone nearby hooted in appreciation, Dante broke the kiss, lifting his head enough for them to see one another. Promises danced in his deep brown eyes and she couldn't look away even if she'd wanted to.

"Stay for the next set," he said, face still inches from hers. "But don't dance with anyone else unless you want me jumping off the stage and reminding you why you're waiting for me."

Mute and breathless, she could only nod. The command in his voice was something she recognized from his way at work, in surgery, and not one piece of her wanted to disobey.

He kissed her again, a soft little kiss as if to seal the deal, then lifted her head back to where it should be. His fingers slid from her hair and stroked down over the back of her head once to right her usually smooth locks, before he returned to the stage.

Oh, she was going to make a mistake. Big mistake.

And it'd be worth it.

Dante hoisted himself onto the stage, bypassing the need to weave past the other musicians to reach his piano. He'd no more sat than the first notes of the next set rang out from the horns to his left.

Thank heaven it was a fast number. His only outlet was his hands right now, and they could only move with the music, not fast enough to deal with the energy surging through him.

From memory, without even needing to think about it by now, he began to play.

For once he didn't fall into that peaceful place where he felt between worlds. His mind didn't blank at all.

It filled with Lise. He couldn't recall the last time anyone had excited him this much.

When he'd first seen her, every drop of blood in his body had hummed, pressure everywhere increasing in a kind of awareness he'd have called supernatural if he wasn't supposed to be a rational surgeon. He'd immediately known there was someone in the club worth seeing.

But his interest—while authentic and entirely sexual—had gotten a little off track when something about her had struck him as familiar. He'd started clicking through the possibilities as to why.

Slept together before? No. That body would be impossible to forget.

Someone who'd been in the club before? No. He'd only owned it for five years, but if he'd ever seen her there, he would've paid attention. Would've gotten her number.

Someone he'd known in his past? One of his former marks? No, she wouldn't have looked at him like that if that was the connection.

Hospital? Family of patient? Staff?

Then it had crystalized.

Bradshaw. This morning's nurse. He'd seen her not even ten hours ago, and would see her again Monday morning. Would she have this magnetic draw hidden in gray cloth and without the sexy makeup and inferno-red lips?

Not if she went home with him tonight—and the way she blushed and smiled said she would. Things could get messy at work. He was already certain she'd not tell his secret, but this might be too big a hope.

The song ended and another began, but he couldn't change his thoughts as easily as he changed keys. He wanted her and that was reason enough to engage in a little after-hours fun.

The eye-roll when she'd spoken of marriage told him she wouldn't take one night out of context. That helped. That made it easy. Why was he still thinking about it?

The lights made it impossible to see her or her table and he wanted to look at her. When the next song rounded out and his hands were free, he snatched a radio from the side, turned away from the crowd. Quietly, he issued an order for Max, Manager of The Inferno, to have the lights lowered to anything but spotlights.

When the lighting shifted to swirls of color over the dance floor, his vision cleared.

Still at the table, he confirmed, but she sat there staring at her phone now, a tiny, satisfied, smug little smile curling one corner of her now naked mouth.

Jefferson had texted back after getting the photo.

Suffering. Good. Just as Dante expected. A little light manipulation of the man who'd humiliated the woman coming home with him tonight. It felt like justice, not that he could really tell the difference between justice and vengeance these days.

Time came for the piano to join in the next song again, and he finally let the music take him. Forty-five more minutes, a half hour break, and then another long set before he could do what he really wanted: drag Lise home with him and peel that dress off her.

While Dante played, Lise's courage started to wane. Her desire was there—had been there all the time, bubbling under the surface of her quiet everyday life—since she'd gotten the job in Neurosurgery. Ignored. Designated unimportant— a luxury, a frivolous, stupid luxury that had no business in her daily life. But it felt different now.

She'd had the lusty crush for years, and it had never caused her insides to quake.

One night could be amazing, or it could lead to life-plan-altering complications.

As much as she wanted him to jump down from the stage, capture her head and kiss her senseless again, what would it do to their work relationship? Had that kiss already changed their work relationship? Would she already be unable to look at him without imagining his hands in her hair and on her bare throat?

She loved her job. She also loved the money—which had enabled her to buy a little cottage of her very own in pricy Miami. Money had gotten her to the first goal on her list of what a responsible woman would do before having a child.

*One kiss could be forgotten.*

*One night with Dante...wasn't worth her future plans.*

The very idea of losing her unconceived child opened a cavern inside her, refining her focus.

Right.

Remember the plan. Even knocking it off schedule was unacceptable, or would be as soon as she selected the best donor and worked out a schedule of some sort.

Who even knew how long or how many tries it might take to get pregnant once she'd found The One from her database?

Good decision.

While she gave herself a mental pep talk, her cell phone buzzed—another message from Jefferson, this time with an ETA.

Dante swung the door of his office closed a little harder than he meant to, knocking a jacket off the hooks on the door. He left it. Max usually spent his evenings on the floor, which suited Dante— it meant he could have solitude in the office they shared whenever Dante wanted.

Lise wasn't there. She hadn't waited, and he'd been so certain she would. Worse, as much as he'd fiddled with her phone earlier tonight, he hadn't gotten her number.

He couldn't remember the last time he'd so misjudged someone. He'd given her exactly what she'd wanted, but she'd left anyway.

Had she left when Jefferson had finally decided to come groveling—something he felt confident he'd accomplished for her? He could check security tapes, but it didn't really matter. Her decision.

He was just angry about effectively being stood up by a woman who wanted him.

The phone in his pocket buzzed, interrupting one of his favorite pastimes—analyzing others—and he fished it out before flinging himself on the leather sofa he occasionally napped on between sets.

This wasn't the emergency ringtone from his answering service or the hospital. He didn't have to answer it right now—it could wait until tomorrow, or later.

One rule governed his time at the club: don't violate the sanctuary. Don't bring the outside in, don't take the inside out. Lise's appearance tonight had completely obliterated his rule.

Turning the screen up, he read a text from the latest Valentino wife—Cassie, married to his twin—with a request for a consult tomorrow at Seaside. His day off, but he never turned down those requests and texted back to confirm.

Lise being there had felt like a violation until he'd been completely turned on by her. But even as the thought came, he knew Lise wasn't the reason he'd answered the text—she didn't have his number either.

Over the past few months he'd watched all his

brothers marry and start families. That was why he'd answered. Why he'd even opened the text after seeing who it was from. They all had bigger lives, which to him meant the possibility more things could go wrong and need fixing. Fixing problems was his primary role in the family.

Wives and kids meant more people to take care of. His circle had expanded from three to seven, with eight and nine still gestating. That kind of serious growth demanded more of his attention—even within the sanctuary.

He must be crazy even thinking about trying to increase those numbers further by finding a wife of his own. Not that he had the first clue as to how to go about it.

Another text came in before he could even drop the phone on the sofa, ripping a sigh from him. He stared at the polished black gadget in his hand for a full minute before he flipped it over and read the next message.

Santiago—middle brother—and his wife Saoirse requested he come to dinner tomorrow.

That one he didn't have it in him to answer right now. Newlyweds. He was surrounded by newlyweds, and he heard from them all far more regularly than he had before they'd all coupled off. Had they organized efforts to take care of him? Because that was how he felt—irritatingly taken care of, the absolute last thing he needed. It would continue until he married. The last Valentino bachelor must be looked after...

The trauma they'd faced in childhood brought that compulsion out in all of them, maybe most in him, but his care had done the job—they were still together enough for him to feel overly tended.

In their shoes, Dante would've been doing the math—he'd never brought a woman to meet them, or dated one woman for any length of time. He'd never given it much thought until they'd all married off, and now he became aware of how he stuck out as single. But marriage was normal, expected. And keeping up appearances was always important.

Dropping the phone on the sofa, he laid his head back and closed his eyes, focusing on the between-sets music that got feet on the dance floor. That had gotten him and Lise on the dance floor.

Someone would knock if he fell asleep before the last set. Or if he lost track of time, fantasizing about stripping Lise of that hot dress.

He just wished he knew her better, knew whether her self-esteem would've let her leave with the man who'd stood her up and insulted her when he'd come groveling.

Jefferson had been easy. Lise, apparently, wasn't as easy to figure out.

Now, what if he wanted to torture her for standing *him* up, make her regret and come groveling...

Monday morning, Dante stood at the scrub bay, looking over the team getting things ready for the morning's surgery.

Lise wasn't there.

He tilted his head to catch sight of the clock, his jaw tightening enough that he had to open his mouth to relieve it. Walking out at the club he could forgive. But being late for surgery?

"Carrasco. *Dónde está* Bradshaw?" The words flew out before he'd even fully realized his irritation. She was never late. What had changed? Just the kiss? Had she gone on another blind date then overslept in her last hurrah?

"Spanish today, Dr. Valentino?" She tilted her head, but answered, "I've not seen her."

Spanish. At work. First time for everything.

It surprised him, but he couldn't even pretend to himself that his irritation was all about her being late. He switched to English—control was important. "Has anyone heard from Bradshaw? She wouldn't no-show."

"I can call HR and scheduling, see if she's called in," Carrasco said.

Although she'd already scrubbed in to prep, and picking up a phone would mean she would have to scrub in again, Dante said, "Do it."

A moment later, she was in the scrub bay, dialing.

Again Thursday's question came: had Lise left with Jefferson?

That was four days ago. If she'd gotten into trouble that long ago...

He fumbled the scrub brush and it fell into the sink. Containing a sigh, he grabbed a new one and started over.

Carrasco spoke with someone, heard her confirm that Lise hadn't called in.

"Not with HR," she confirmed, and dialed another number.

He didn't want another surgical nurse for this procedure. Lise was the best. He wanted Lise. Carrasco technically was also a surgical nurse, but he had Lise for today, it was on the schedule.

"I'm here!"

The sound of Lise's voice had him turning from

the sink, relief tinging his irritation so that he didn't quite know how to feel, which of course ticked him off. "Couldn't get out of bed this morning, Bradshaw?"

He took in her appearance, and he felt his neck heat. The too-big scrub top she always wore had been replaced by one with a different cut—one that wrapped over her chest like that dress had done.

She'd made the gray scrubs sexy.

"Nothing so restful as that." She rushed around the small bay, getting what she'd need to start scrubbing. "I know I'm a little later than usual, but we're still a good fifteen minutes from the start of the surgery..."

Dante didn't want excuses. He also didn't want to cause a scene at the hospital, even if she threw him off balance yet again. He wanted Old Lise, not the one who knocked him so hard she had him wondering if maybe he was the mark here.

She stepped to the open bay beside him and began the process of cleaning her hands.

Hair covered by scrub cap—how he always saw her. No makeup—but no lower face cover yet. He'd like the chance to look at her clean-faced—or grill her for an excuse. But it would have to wait.

If she hadn't wanted to face him after their brief time at The Inferno, he'd put that straight to her. No reason they couldn't be professional. It had been a little kissing, not as much as he admittedly still wanted, but they'd survive.

He exited the bay, leaving the nurses to finish scrubbing in. Another tech gowned and gloved him, and he took a moment to make sure everything was as he wanted before the patient arrived.

"Are you going to report in about your date last week?" another member of the team asked as soon as Lise stepped into the OR proper.

"No. It's really not the time for that. If you want a report, I will be happy to make one after surgery."

Voice tight. Posture stiff. Happy? Yeah, right. No way could he misread that reaction.

He just didn't know whether it was Jefferson or their dancing making her unhappy now.

If the date had shown up he hadn't made a better impression on her. Unless it was their dalliance making her unhappy.

What the devil was wrong with him? He'd never had this much trouble reading someone. At least, not since those early days on the cons that had almost gotten him arrested in his youth. Repetition had improved how well he could read between the lines, except when it came to Lise.

The door opened and in rolled the trolley with his patient on it, a woman in her thirties who had three children.

That was what he needed to focus on, doing well by this patient and her family. Never be the one who broke a family.

He always learned what he could about his patients so he could keep in mind what was riding on successful surgery. He took a moment to check with her, make sure she understood what the neuro-endoscopy entailed, and to reassure her again that he'd do his best. Things he always did for his patients, even those who didn't have children at home or in the waiting room—or, as had been the case with him, waiting in the chapel, praying it all would go all right.

His gentle encouraging words delivered, he nodded to the anesthetist. The sooner their patient was unconscious, the sooner she'd stop worrying. And, he hoped, the sooner he'd have out the Rathke cleft cyst growing behind her pituitary gland.

One more tally removed from the ledger where

he kept memories of his old ways, and he hoped to eventually get out of the red.

No sooner had Dante left the surgical suite than Sandy Carrasco repeated her earlier demand.

"Tell us how the date went."

Lise had avoided thinking about the date all weekend, and that had included preparing what she was going to say when inevitably asked.

"Oh, just great, I guess." Messing with rude people was a bad habit she'd apparently picked up from Dante.

When Sandy laughed, Lise went with it.

"I got a brand-new dress for the evening. Jefferson and I had spoken briefly on the phone a few days before and confirmed where we'd meet in texts—deciding on a club he liked. Since I never go to clubs, I got the new red dress. I arrived, went in on my own as he wasn't waiting for me outside. Drank a mojito. Danced."

"He was inside, waiting?"

"Oh, no. He wasn't there, either. I amused myself. Mojitos. Dancing. Talking with a handsome musician." Not. Dante. Don't mention Dante. Then she laid out being stood up, the Large Woman nonsense, and that he'd tried to come after she'd sent him a picture of her red dress.

Confrontation wasn't usually her thing, though it sometimes came with being truthful and direct about things—or when humiliated and inebriated. But sometimes, like right now, it came in handy.

Before Sandy could do anything but look embarrassed, Lise—having already discarded her surgical gown—gestured to the new well-fitted scrub top and her relatively flat tummy and waist.

"I'm not tiny. But I'm pretty sure Large doesn't describe me. I tend to wear a ten in scrub bottoms and, of course, a higher size when I require a cut that accommodates disproportionate breasts. And before you get any ideas, I'm still counting that as my third date, so that's only…"

She paused then and revulsion for the whole experience changed her mind. "Whoever was in charge of picking Bachelors Four and Five should cancel now. I'm done. Be disapproving all you like, but my plans don't hinge on whether or not my coworkers approve of my decisions. And now, I apparently need to go be yelled at by Dr. Valentino. Please excuse me."

# CHAPTER THREE

THE DOOR TO the office Dante used when staffing the neurosurgery unit swung open. He looked up just as he flipped off his phone, and caught Lise closing the door behind her.

Brows pushed together, mouth actually turning down at the corners in a frown, posture stiff, hands balled into fists... She was either very angry or very worried.

Something other than unflappably calm for the first time ever in his presence at Buena Vista, but she'd also embraced another first—at least as far as he was concerned: No scrub cap. The silky blond locks he'd spent the weekend remembering the feel of on his hand had been braided around her head like a crown. She didn't keep her hair just tucked up beneath those caps. Still nice.

But not what he should be focusing on.

She stepped in front of the chairs opposite the desk, appeared to think better of it, and moved around until she stood behind them again and dropped her hands onto the seatback.

Rather than question her, he let her get around to it. She knew why he'd summoned her.

When words again failed to come, she stepped around to the front again, but this time sat.

"Do you have a cat?" he asked, unable to help himself.

"Because I'm unmarried and twenty-nine? How many cats am I supposed to have at this point?"

"You just walked all the way around that chair about one and a half times before you sat down. My guess was either cat or a musical-chairs aficionado."

"You're funny today." Yet she neither looked nor sounded amused.

"I was funny on Thursday too. You should've stuck around to find out."

"If you said anything funny on Thursday, it would've been in some kind of Spanish purr and I wouldn't have understood it anyway."

Quiet Lise had been once more replaced by a snarky copy. She was there to entertain him, it seemed. But he had a plan for this meeting, so he moved past the cat conversation.

"Are you all right? You looked anxious when

you came in. Afraid I was going to yell at you for your tardiness?"

"A little. And I just told off Sandy and called off the remaining fix-ups. Told them I didn't need their approval to live my life. It was really...I don't know, either empowered or rude. Maybe both."

"Sometimes you have to be rude to get things done," Dante murmured, leaning back in the other chair as he tried to decide how to handle this.

"You didn't need to be rude to get things done." Her phone.

"I didn't know you well enough to trust you." Getting off track.

"You've worked with me for two years."

"And yet I barely know you."

Rarely did he ever do anything in his adult life without having a plan for how it should work out. That was how he'd gotten through the time after his parents' murders, through college and medical school, fellowships, even to securing a placement at his preferred hospital. His career path still had an ongoing plan. He had plans for the club, and a great manager to make those plans happen. The only goal he was flying blind with was on how to go about finding a wife with his particular marital complications.

It was time he had his own family. And he had to marry if he was to have a happy family.

Lise had a habit of disrupting his plans. When he'd gone to her table at first, his plan had been simple: find out what she knew and make sure she didn't tell anyone about The Inferno. That plan had lasted all of two minutes.

He'd formed a new plan for the way that evening should've ended as they'd danced and the chemistry had grown, and that hadn't worked out either.

When he'd instructed she come to his office, he'd been planning to demand answers to her tardiness—mostly to make sure she hadn't overslept after a long sexy weekend with the jerk who'd stood her up.

"Why did you stand me up?" he asked.

And another plan went down the drain. Probably not the best use of a work environment, but his plan to keep his work and his club completely separate had also blazed out when Lise had walked into it in that dress. Besides, how else was he supposed to figure her out but to ask questions?

She looked momentarily confused again, but embarrassed too. "I didn't think you wanted those places to cross-contaminate each other. Am I supposed to call you Dante or Dr. Valentino right now?"

"Dante," he answered immediately—he liked it when she said his name. "I didn't want it, but it happened anyway."

"You sexy-danced with me and sang Spanish into my ear. That's not just something that happens." Her voice had gone up, the same as when she'd yelled at him about being rude in the club. She might not plan to behave differently in the club and in the hospital, but she did.

"You being there happened. Everything that came afterward was a choice, and nothing I regret." He cleared that up, so she couldn't think he was blaming her for his apparently clumsy seduction. "So, why did you leave?"

"So I wouldn't sleep with you."

"Why? You wanted to. You wanted a last hurrah. I'd guaranteed a last hurrah without complications."

She all but rolled her eyes at him. "It's easy to say no complications, but it would've messed everything up. It's already messing things up, and all we did was dance and kiss."

Dante scooted his chair toward her, then grabbed the arms of her chair to drag her to face him.

She made a face as her chair slid on the carpet, a flash of pain that gave him pause. But it was gone as fast as it had come, so he tried to stay on plan—the new plan, the one that had re-formed without his reasoned intention a moment ago.

"This right now is only awkward because you ran out. Did you think I would force you to do something you didn't want?"

"No. I wanted it. But it was a bad decision, fueled by mojitos and hormones and because, well, I've been lonely, if you must know. And you're very handsome, and then there was the dancing and the sexy stuff you said in Spanish." She blew out a breath slowly and reached up to rub her face.

She looked just as frustrated as he was. "If you're going to storm into single motherhood, you need to get better at handling social interactions. In the future, you can just say, 'Thanks, but I changed my mind.'"

"Thanks, but I changed my mind," she repeated, but, despite the sarcastic repetition of his words, not an ounce of it rang in her voice.

"Cute." He reached out and snagged one of her hands to force her to focus on him—contact with another had a great side benefit of granting the appearance of trustworthiness, and he needed an advantage with her. "I was actually worried about you. Something you'll become familiar with as a single parent, trust me."

"What were you worried for?" She didn't pull away, but her arm had a stiffness that spoke of inner turmoil, and when she met his gaze he felt the balance shift.

"I saw your face during the set. You were smirking at your cell phone. WonderDate texted you back."

"WonderDate?" she repeated, and then grinned despite herself. "He did. But don't call him that—he'd have to have shown up to be any kind of wonder. In fact, I didn't even text him back. You were worried that he'd come for me and I just forgave all and ran off with him?"

"You'd had at least three mojitos, and I'd been doing my best to seduce you, so it was possible I'd contributed to you making a bad decision."

Mild exasperation had her shaking her head at him, even though she still didn't pull her hand away. "He texted several times after getting the picture. I never answered. When he finally texted that he was on his way and would be there well before your set ended, I decided to get out before I did anything stupid."

"Explain stupid." He kept her hand, kept looking her in the eye. It had a double benefit, as he also got to look at her clean-faced, and the pale blue eyes drew his own gaze.

"You know what stupid is. Stupid is what we were doing. What we were going to do. What we might be doing now!" She wriggled her hand out of his, but the buzzing connection he'd felt lingered.

"That wasn't stupid. That would've been a much-desired reprieve from reality for a while. You feel it." He gestured to her freed hand. "I know you do."

"It's just chemistry. It doesn't mean that the rest disappears."

He caught both her hands and stilled, holding her wary gaze while the buzz resumed and morphed to a persistent tingle that either required more touching or none at all.

More.

Dante leaned forward, elbows on his knees, and brought one small hand to his lips to brush a kiss across her knuckles, then turned it until it was palm up, and feathered a trail of kisses from the center of her palm to the tender inside of her wrist.

Her breathing changed, and when he lifted his

eyes to hers again, her mouth was open and she had that excited haze settling in her eyes again.

"That connection you feel? Sex with us would be like that—intense and hot. It's kind of silly that we're still talking about this when we both know it's going to happen."

"You don't know that." She breathed, blinking her eyes and pulling her hand free, gently but firmly. She knew it too, but she didn't want to know it. Why, though, he couldn't fathom. "And what did you mean before?"

"When?"

"When you said that I would know about worry," Lise said, grabbing for anything to chase away the charge in the air. Today had been far from her image of a great day at work. It had started out badly, she'd dropped instruments in surgery and new ones had had to be broken out of their sterile packaging. Twice. She never dropped instruments. Now every cell in her body was zinging and she wanted more contact with his skin, with his lips... She wanted to dance, she wanted to argue with him more—probably the weirdest part of the compulsion she felt to engage with him.

The sooner they got past this, the better it would

be—as it was, she struggled to resist that sensation, which turned it into that need, that near ache.

Being a sarcastic witch had always been helpful in persuading men that she was entirely not worth the effort, but so far, not Dante. "Is that an implication you worried about me like a parent?"

Lise sat up straighter in her chair, then regretted it. Her neck and right shoulder had started to ache from the accident this morning, and sitting up straighter just put added tension on those muscles.

"I've been a parent. I know what it is to worry. And," he said, mirroring her actions, sitting up but taking it a step further with folded arms, "in no way do I feel parent-like toward you."

"You have kids?" The image of her ducky nursery swam into her mind.

"Had. Younger siblings. I raised them with my brother when our parents were murdered."

*When our parents were murdered.*

The words curdled deep in her belly, but she didn't see even a trace of emotion on his handsome face.

In surgery, she could read his eyes—she had a context and two years' practice interpreting his looks to make that possible. Now? His expression had gone as blank and as unaffected as his voice had been.

An innate desire to help and heal had made her become a nurse, but this was so big and his words were so heavy that she couldn't even focus on them. Shifting sand, that's what it was like to speak with the man. No direction ever looked safe, but plodding directly for what had to still be a wound felt the least safe.

Talk about the kids. "How old are they?"

"Now or then?"

"Then." Though she doubted he'd entirely given up those parental feelings, no matter how old they all were now.

"Alejandro is youngest, he was ten. Santiago was fourteen. Rafe and I were eighteen."

"You have a twin? You mean there're *two* of you?" She nudged his foot with her toe and settled her foot beside his, shoes touching when all she really wanted to do was reach for his hand again, and…what? It had been a long time ago.

"Fraternal. Not identical." He smiled, but despite the little tease he didn't say anything else.

What comfort could she offer after all these years?

He hadn't told her because he wanted comfort.

Of course it still hurt—she could summon the shock and anguish of losing her father in an instant, but that was different. His had been a double-whammy violence perpetrated by others, not them simply deciding to die.

There was something else he'd meant. Her plan. "You think I'm making a mistake going forward with my pregnancy plan because I have no family."

That surprised him. That expression she could identify. He really didn't know anything about her, so why it surprised him, she couldn't guess.

"You have no family?" Alarm. Identified. "No one at all?"

Great.

Lise sighed. This had gotten too far off track, and she didn't know how to get it back on track. Not with her contradictory reaction to wanting him, and his single-minded focus on tempting her—either physically or emotionally.

They barely knew one another, even if she knew one really terrible thing from his past. "It doesn't matter. I'm not going to let the fact that I don't have a family keep me from having a family. Don't go down that road."

A knock at the door cut off whatever he'd been

about to say. Dante stood up, one of his knees between hers, his body so fleetingly close it dominated her personal space and pulled at her like gravity—so like that moment after the kiss to end all kisses, when he'd stood over her, hand fisted in her hair, and the pull between them so strong other people in the club had felt it.

Her tongue stuck to the roof of her mouth and she felt herself craning forward to look up at him, but a shot of pain radiated down her right arm. She lowered her chin again and he stepped around to head for the door.

"Hello, Dr. Valentino. I wanted to check in and see if you'd heard from Lise Bradshaw? Do you want to file disciplinary action against her?" a woman's voice asked from the other side of the door, sounding entirely too cheerful considering the words she'd chosen.

Disciplinary action?

Who was that? Human Resources?

She tilted her head to try and see past him, but Dante's body blocked the small opening in the door.

"She arrived just after we hung up with you earlier. No need for disciplinary action. This was her first tardiness, and she had a very good excuse."

They hadn't even talked about why she'd been late. Was the man allergic to the truth?

He spoke with her a moment longer, then added a doozy. "But it's good you stopped by. I want to start paperwork to have Nurse Bradshaw transferred to my team full time."

He gave reasons—not all entirely true, but mostly. They came to some kind of agreement, and Dante closed the door and returned to sit with her.

"How do you know I had a good excuse? I haven't told you anything about why I was late."

"You're not the tardy sort." His phone rang and he held up one finger, checked the screen, and said, "It's Recovery. I've got them giving me updates every twenty minutes."

So he'd assumed, which was different from lying how? Not at all. She could have a terrible excuse for all he knew.

For the most part Lise was confident in her personal life. She might not have been had she known her fellow nurses were judging her for the size of her scrub tops, but generally she felt confident in her abilities, her job, her life plans, her moral compass...

But she wasn't so confident as to assume she knew everything. Did unreasonable confidence make something not a lie?

Another reason she should run the other direction. Dante hadn't even *asked* if she wanted a full transfer to his team, he'd just started the ball rolling.

Dante rang off and dropped the phone back into his chest pocket. "So, you were saying?"

"I was asking why you just lied, because you never asked why I was late."

"No one will question it. Our secret, then? I was simply giving you the benefit of the doubt."

"I don't like secrets. And you admit you had doubts." Lecturing a grown man about honesty wasn't a smart use of her time, and yet…prior to this morning Lise would've never thought she could enjoy arguing with anyone, and she really didn't want to examine why she liked arguing with him.

"You're right. Tell me why you were tardy."

"Because I was rear-ended this morning on the way to work," she said. "Which, granted, is a good excuse. But the point is—"

"You had a car accident on the way to work?"

He cut her off—much as the driver ahead of her had done, which had ended in her being rear-ended. "You had an accident and you were only about fifteen minutes later than usual? Did you have yourself checked out? That's why you were dropping instruments and why you keep rubbing your shoulder?"

Muttering an expletive, he didn't wait for her to answer the questions at all, just stood, rounded her chair, and ran his fingers along her vertebrae. Thumb. It was the pad of his thumb—she could even feel the texture of his skin, the ripple of every ridge of his thumbprint seemed to stand out to her.

The man went from smirking and self-assured to angry doctor mode in an instant. She couldn't keep up, and moments before smirking and self-assured, he'd been all sexy.

"I'm a little sore. It didn't destroy my car. They didn't have to cut me out with the Jaws of Life. My back bumper fell off. I got a jar forward but I'm okay. I'm just a little sore."

"A little sore deserves to be checked out." He swore again and once again one hand slipped around the front of her neck, long index finger and thumb cradling the underside of her mandible while his palm and fingers cupped her throat.

"What are you doing?"

"I'm keeping you from—stop moving your head!" he grumbled, and then he was speaking again—no doubt into the phone since he wasn't talking to her.

"My neck isn't broken."

Radiology. He was calling Radiology. She didn't know what to feel, amused or aggravated. "I don't need any imaging done."

"You might have whiplash. You might have something that would benefit from immobilization, and you're flouncing around like you haven't a care in the world."

"I didn't flounce!" She tried to look up at him again and Dante dropped his phone in her lap so he could get a better hold on her neck.

"I was late for work. We performed the surgery and then I came right to you here, as you demanded. When was I supposed to get checked out? If I called you and said, 'Oh, Dr. Valentino, I think I may need to see a doctor. I feel moderately frowny on the picture pain scale, is it okay if I blow off your neuro-endoscopy?' you would've lost your mind."

This kind of conversation had never happened with him prior to last week. She'd always been her professional, antiseptic work self before—keeping her work environment calm. She liked calm and safe, she lived for calm and safe—something she'd never been able to control in the middle section of her life. Or even before a year ago when she'd finally stopped living in crappy apartments in crappier neighborhoods so she could save down-payment money for her cottage.

With one hand, he grabbed his phone off her thigh and dialed again. He'd stopped listening again. And now he had in-hospital transport com-ing—someone with a wheelchair—and a cervical collar sized medium.

"Shut up, Lise," he grumbled, keeping his hand resting against the side of her neck. "You just told me that you don't have any family looking out for you or making you take care of yourself. So, you're going to have some X-rays, and if they're fine, you can just go home and rest for the remainder of the day. Though really you should prob-ably at least schedule a massage, because today you're a little sore, tomorrow you're going to be very sore."

"I'm not that fragile."

"But you *are* that stubborn."

"I'm just so glad we're not blowing things out of proportion."

# CHAPTER FOUR

"WOW, BRADSHAW, YOU look worse than I expected."

Dante stood on the other side of Lise's front door, several shopping bags in hand, saying the words every woman longed to hear from the man she no longer secretly lusted after.

"So maybe my neck locked up this morning. And maybe my shoulder is also refusing to function without shocking pain. And maybe I have to pivot at the waist like a robot to fling the door open. But do we need to have another talk about rudeness?" She stuck there in the doorway, not yet inviting him in but not even doubting that her stink-eye had lost efficacy with her inability to look him in the eye without tilting her body and twisting to the side.

"No, all you have to do is say, 'Dante, my friend, you were right to be concerned for me after my accident.'" He put his bag-laden arms out and stepped forward, the motion causing her to instinctively move out of his way.

Ignoring his demand, she turned to head for the kitchen. "Gloating is unattractive. Please tell me they let you pick up the prescriptions." She trekked stiffly toward the kitchen, expecting him to follow.

"You should be more hospitable to your white knight," he said, but she heard the door close and lock, then his footfalls following behind her.

"I'll be very nice as soon as you produce my feel-better prescriptions."

He stopped at her counter and carefully dumped the bags onto the clean surface, then picked up a small paper bag and rattled it. "The prescriptions you wouldn't have if...?"

"You hadn't picked them up for me." She said the words he wanted, even though her pride already smarted from having had to ask for help at all. More than that, she'd looked forward to him coming round for more reasons than her prescription delivery. Her job kept her sane, and she only noticed it when she was actually confined away from people—no one to talk to.

She reached for the bag, but he pulled it out of her pitiful reach.

"And?"

"If you hadn't forced me to get checked out yesterday. Are you happy now?" Lise snatched the small bag, triggering a flash of pain up her shoulder and neck.

"Happy might be overstating it. You're certainly in a bad mood, though." He gathered up perishables to put into the fridge.

Less than a minute later, and with the aid of a straw in her water glass, Lise got the pills down.

As soon as she set her glass on the counter, a half-peeled banana was pressed into her hand. "You know better than to take anti-inflammatories on an empty stomach. Eat that, unless you want to feel worse in about a half hour."

She took a grumbling bite of the banana without giving in to her grouchy urge to yell at him about everything. Bad mood didn't really cover how grouchy she felt today, and how much it had ratcheted up since he'd arrived—and this despite having been looking forward to it. So, great, now she'd lost her mind, not just her ability to look to the left.

The man had done nothing to earn her ire today either. He hadn't crashed into her. He'd gone out of his way to call and check on her this morning, and was the only reason she should experience some relief shortly.

*In the future, even if you don't think you'll need them, fill the darned prescription.*

*And consider saying thank you.*

"You may have squirrels nesting in the back of your hair." His playful tone softened her irritation a little, but her fire deserting her just left a glum feeling behind.

"I can't brush it effectively, and I was asleep on the sofa before you got here. Sexy, right?"

"I would've said cute, but you're so grouchy that it kind of negates the cute factor." He reached over and finger-combed it down a little, the gentle touch warming her.

She could lean against him and soak up a little comfort, and she suddenly really wanted to. Dumb. Dumb not to keep this budding friendship from going further.

"I can brush it out for you if you like."

The thought of him brushing her hair suddenly felt too intimate. Especially standing in the kitchen of her cottage.

That feeling snowballed when she saw the pink box he discretely shuffled off to the side of his purchases.

Tampons.

Her stomach dropped and she almost choked on her banana. "I forgot about those…"

Why had she asked him to buy them?

Because she'd been annoyed about him being right.

Because she didn't want him to feel too pleased with himself about her needing his assistance.

Because she didn't want it to be easy to accept future help, and thought they might make him think twice before offering.

Because she'd reasoned he could interpret the request as 'Stay Away!'

"Tell me how much I owe you for all this."

Dante looked at her sideways. "Don't worry about it. Even if you were, what? Testing me?"

"No. A little. Mostly I've been miserable and angry, and I thought it would encourage you to deliver stuff and leave, not grow roots. It was immature, but you don't know how annoying it is to take care of yourself for practically your whole life and then suddenly not be able to. And you've been so…" she stepped over to the table for her purse, dug into it and came out with her phone "…weirdly nice. It makes me suspicious. Tell me the amount and your email address so I can transfer funds."

Not part of his plan. Friends didn't need to be reimbursed, so he ignored the subject.

He took the phone away from her, put it on the table, and put his arm around her back to steer her toward the living room. "I have you scheduled to work with me on Thursday, and it's not an easy surgery, so you can be assured that I'm here for selfish reasons. I need you in that surgery, and unmedicated." A hint of truth there, but not entirely. He had a new plan regarding Lise. "So, have you scheduled a massage?"

He walked her all the way to the sofa and stepped back, indicating she should sit, which she did, the disgruntled tangle-haired, stiff-necked beauty letting go of some of the anger that seemed to be fueling her today. If she could use her spine currently, he'd call her pliant.

"I did, but I can't get in to see anyone until tomorrow afternoon. And if it's this bad tomorrow, I don't think that having a single massage twelve hours before surgery will be that helpful. You might want to schedule someone else, or just wait until Thursday and hand off to Sandy if I discover I still can't perform."

"Or you could let me have a go at it. I can't make it any worse." He sat beside her and leaned back into the large, plush cushions. As he sank in, his mind went temporarily blank. So much better than his sofa...

"So, this is all about work." It should've been a question, but the way she said it, it became a dubious statement.

"Work, and I was concerned about you, which I was right to be." He looked toward her, then leaned forward to keep the cushions from swallowing him.

"But you wouldn't have been before."

True. "I wouldn't have known you were completely alone before. Do you even have friends to call in case of emergency?"

She flinched, and took her time shifting around on the sofa until she sat sideways, her legs crossed, able to look at him. "Not close friends here. I have some in Jacksonville."

"Hometown?"

"Yes."

"Why haven't you made any friends but me since you've been here?"

"You really classify yourself as my friend? I thought your main goal was sex."

"And getting you in to work on Thursday. But I can do all three." Her eyes went a little bleary and he knew how tired she was. "Why don't you have any friends in Miami?"

She was likeable enough when not in such a grouchy mood. Funny. Sarcastic. As enjoyable as anyone he'd ever met, but genuine too. Smart. Sexy. The more time he spent with her, the better he knew her. She had strong morals, but wasn't holier than thou about it. She responded to emotion and others' pain every time.

To get her to agree to be his wife—he was increasingly certain she was the right choice—that's where he had to lead her. Emotions. Empathy. Not pity inspired, but because he'd have to make clear to her that he was better than a sperm donor. Lise was the solution to his marriage problem. He just had to get her to come around to his way of thinking without scaring her off. She could already walk without difficulty in both of his worlds.

All she had to do was accept him as the better option.

"I have friends, just none that I feel comfortable asking for favors. I never ask people to take care of me. I'm the one who takes care of others. I wouldn't have asked you for anything if you hadn't called and offered. And if I didn't desperately need that medicine."

The little diatribe exposed a lot, but he didn't want to make her feel worse about that—at least, not yet. All information could have value to him, but should only be used when most beneficial.

"I'm your friend," he said, then added, "The others are acquaintances, not friends." He leaned back into cushions, even if they pulled him in and made him relax when he should be putting his best face forward—not getting too comfortable.

No answer came immediately, but the way her eyes skirted the empty space said she was thinking about something.

"It's hard to get to know people as you get older. Everyone my age seems to have settled down and started a family, they don't have the time it takes to get to know someone well enough to become a really good friend."

"It is hard. I don't have many good friends either." But he didn't need extra people in his life to fill a void. He had two voids left: wife and children.

"I'm here and willing to put in the time. But we have some things to work on first." He forced himself to sit forward. "Do you feel the muscle relaxers yet?"

Lise carefully turned her head a small amount, then confirmed, "It's a little better." She leaned a little to watch as he stood up and gestured to the rest of the sofa.

"Lie down on your belly." He offered her a hand to help, and if he didn't already understand how badly her neck hurt, he'd have figured it out when she took his hands and let him guide and help her flat.

"This isn't going to turn into something sexy, is it? Because I really don't think I can handle that right now. I'm drugged. And my head is starting to feel like gelatin."

"Nothing sexy. I'd put you on your back if I was going for a sexy massage." Especially in those pajamas. Tank top. No bra. Short shorts. The only thing that could shut his libido down right now was knowing she was in pain.

She laughed a little, and gingerly he shifted her arms down to her sides. There had to be an easy-to-find hairbrush in the bathroom, and it could only help to get her to relax first.

"Where are you going?"

"Just a second."

He returned with it a moment later and sat beside her.

"If you found sensual massage oils, I'm calling off Thursday."

Ignoring that, he reached for her hair and began gently working that tangle out. A groan came out as he worked his way to the scalp and the bristles finally touched down to stroke the skin.

"Feel nice?"

"Yeah. Wasn't expecting it. This is supposed to be my job, though." She'd begun to mumble a little, but he couldn't take credit for it yet. The medication. "Nurse stuff. I may credit the sofa with my recovery, or you may need to blame it on me falling asleep. I like my furniture to suck all aspirations out of me."

He didn't interrupt her sofa babbling, just let her talk while he worked the brush through her hair until it was smooth and tangle free, then gathered the heavy silk into a bunch, twisted it, and laid it over the far shoulder, out of the way. "You can accept a little tending for once. It won't kill you."

"I guess," she mumbled. "As long as we never speak of this. I can't have people knowing my dirty secrets."

Teasing. A good sign.

Lise had experienced more emotional swings in the cumulative two or three hours she'd spent alone with Dante than she had in the last ten years. Having someone check on her made her feel safe. The way he looked at her made her feel sexy—a feeling she'd forgotten when she'd starting wearing the big scrubs and men stopped hitting on her. She still didn't know if Saturday had seen her picking out new scrubs because she didn't want to be invisible any more, or just so Dante would keep looking at her like that.

"Who don't you want to find out you're human?"

As he spoke, he began walking his thumbs up the vertebrae of her neck and then along the overly tensed *trapezius* muscle, gradually increasing the strength with which he manipulated her knotted flesh until it finally started to relax.

The pain started out at the far end of bad, but as he worked, it began to lessen, and she began to drift.

What had he asked her?

*Oh, right.*

"Is that why you hide in the club?"

"No." He pressed on either side of her spine further down and rotated. "And redirecting isn't an answer."

"Everyone, I guess," she said, then lay there, perplexed. Strange answer. The world wasn't afraid of her ability to persevere in the face of adversity. The only one who needed to be constantly convinced she could do whatever she set her mind to was herself. She gave herself regular pep talks about problems that cropped up. She really needed another on why letting Dante get close could be very dumb.

Instead, she was dressing better and letting him into her house. The safer thing would be to cut ties and minimize the effect he had on her. He seemed trustworthy at times, but he was a great actor.

Unlike her.

She wasn't alone in Miami because it was hard to get to know someone well enough to become close—even if that was true too. She could've found people willing and able to make that connection, but she hadn't tried. She was alone in Miami because she avoided letting people get close to her so they couldn't hurt her. She made sure men ignored her by hiding aspects of her appearance that attracted attention—her curves in baggy clothes, and her long blonde hair in practical braids and under caps.

Until the loneliness had overwhelmed her to

the point that she'd agreed to blind dates and had bought that red dress—the only thing that had gotten Dante's attention.

Which she should remember—the dress had gotten his attention, good reason to avoid it. So why wasn't she?

Because…she liked to talk to him, even if her wanting friendships didn't mean she could trust herself to choose good ones. It had never worked out. It never had worked that way for her. Not once. Her friendships in Jacksonville had been nice, but she'd still held people at a distance. The whole history of her personal relationships was littered with liars and manipulators, and she was just the dope who continually fell for it, like she wanted to fall for this.

Dante wasn't this nice. There had to be something he wanted, and she wasn't going to be fooled again.

"Are you up for this?" Dante asked the second Lise joined him in the scrub bay. She looked different. He took a moment to look at her with a critical—not just appreciative—eye.

She adjusted her cap, tucking wispy blonde hairs up under the elastic band, seeming to have full movement of both arms. "I'm doing much better and haven't taken a muscle relaxer since an hour before my massage yesterday. So about fourteen hours ago."

"That's not an answer," Dante said. "Mind doing a range demonstration for me?"

"Do I mind?" Lise repeated, and then chuckled. "Are you sure *you're* up to the surgery, Dr. Valentino?"

It had been a request. Why had it been a request? He didn't make requests in his OR.

"I was trying to curb this rudeness I've been repeatedly told I have," he lied easily. Better she think it was on purpose rather than something he'd have to examine later. "Range of motion," he prompted, pausing in his scrubbing in to watch her. Should've said his deference was due to their friendship, if he'd thought of it, but he was somewhat out of practice actively maneuvering people to do what he wanted. It had been years since he'd worked a long con, and these days he mostly used those old rusty skills to lead patients to better treatment.

Moving a step away for space, she stretched her arms out to the sides, moved them up and down jumping jacks style, then repeated the motion with her arms to the front. Finally, she rotated them at the shoulder and at different heights.

"Pain? Numbness?"

"Sore." She answered that directly at least. "But not worse than a bruised feeling. If you'd rather Sandy take my place, I understand completely."

He didn't even need to think about that one. She was as fit as he could hope at this point, and Lise even at ninety percent was better than anyone else at one hundred percent.

"No. We're draining and debriding a cerebral abscess in a tricky place. I want you."

She joined him at the sink, not commenting on his statement, but the look she gave him reflected his double meaning right back to him.

With no one else in the bay with them, Dante let himself look at her long enough to summon her gaze again, then murmured, "I'm playing tonight. Just me, not the whole band."

Her pale blue eyes widened and darted around until she was satisfied they were alone and not about to be overheard. "Are you inviting me?"

Dante made a sound of affirmation. "But I'd settle for dinner Friday at my house, if you're not up for dancing tonight. You're sore and all."

Soaped to the elbows, outside the frequent looks

around to be sure they continued to be alone, she kept scrubbing and her eyes off him, voice low. "What kind of music is it?"

"Just piano. Whatever I want, but often touching down in the style you heard before."

He didn't need to look, he'd been keeping secrets so long he'd developed an almost supernatural ability to recognize when his surroundings changed. They were still alone. Despite the window separating the bay from the OR, and the people setting up there who could see them talking.

He let himself look at her again. "I'm trying not to demand you do both. Tuesday was the best time I ever had with a grouchy, bratty, whiplash victim. And I promised to put in the time to build a friendship."

The smile that split her face was a reward for his teasing. "Will there be time for talking at the club?" she asked, then teased, "Maybe just dinner. I don't know if I could do two nights with you out of four."

"You could," he murmured, shifting the scrub brush back to his fingernails for a final pass. "You could do many more, but dinner at my house is a good start."

"Don't get ahead of yourself. We always argue,

and I'm not sure if that's what makes great friends." Pink little ears bent outward from the thickness of the scrub cap behind them, leaving her looking like an adorable little elf. A sunburned little elf, perhaps, especially with the way that flush was spreading.

"That's not all we do, but fire is fire, Bradshaw." He rinsed and stepped on the pedal to turn off the water in his sink. "Time for focus. We can talk more later."

One of the nurses met Dante as he came in, gloving and gowning him, then tying his mask around his neck so it could be pulled up later.

"Who's going to get Mr. Polluck? He's in the hyperbaric chamber."

# CHAPTER FIVE

Two days later, Lise stood at the open French doors leading off Dante's living room to a veranda and the spectacular view of the ocean beyond.

The house—or what she'd seen of it—was exactly what she'd expect from him. Modern. Clean lines. Beautiful. But the only parts that looked lived in were these doors, and the baby grand piano situated directly to the right of the doors, where he could no doubt sit, play, and watch the tide.

The bedroom, which she hadn't seen, probably could be included in the lived-in designation—no one could sleep on that sofa. He really did need some furniture that would suck all aspirations out of him. It all likely cost an arm and a leg, but looked like it was made out of hard black plastic. She hadn't tried it, but it was all stacked rectangles and corners—like show room or dollhouse furniture.

Nothing for comfort. It felt like a stage.

When her family had lived in luxury, had it felt so cold and unnatural?

She tried to think back, but couldn't quite grasp a memory of the house that didn't involve the blood and viscera of her loved ones. Everything before that night had gone into some kind of mental black hole, and anything beyond that event horizon felt like someone else's life.

He really needed new furniture. If he was so bent on befriending her—as he continuously claimed—she should be able to tell him that. No one could be happy in this house.

She stuck by the veranda doors.

Dante had busied himself in the kitchen, frying plantains to go with the sandwiches they'd picked up on the way, or she assumed he was cooking in there. The sweet, buttery scent she'd usually associate with the fruit frying didn't reach her over the clean salt air blowing through the doors, and she couldn't tear herself away from the dimming summer sky painted in shades of pink and purple. The sun didn't have to set over the water to make it beautiful and serene—at least one part of his house could do that aspiration-sucking.

"It's nice out here," Dante said from behind her,

then stepped around, that scent she'd been waiting for trailing after him.

Small talk. Maybe that would give her some idea of how to handle this date? Dinner with a friend? She should just try to keep things from getting flirtatious, not worry about anything else. Talk. Eat. Be pleasant. Enjoy the beach and the sound of the ocean. If he talks about something interesting again, even better. But don't let things get sexy.

"Nice isn't a good enough word. But if you put a sofa like mine right here, or some equally comfortable patio furniture out here, all aspirations might blow away in a sea breeze."

He had a tray loaded with dinner and stopped at a small breakfast table, leaving her to trail after him and help him unload the tray.

"Drinks?"

"Margaritas." He dragged a chair out for her and she sat. "Not as good as Mad Ron's, but I did my best."

"That's a funny name for a bar. It's also funny that you go to a bar for the food."

"Best Helibanas you've ever had."

"That'll be easy—I've never had one." She sat

when the tray had been emptied, and reached for the drink.

"Think a Cuban with a couple of tweaks in seasonings and toppings."

An hour later, after the point that the sky had gone midnight blue and the only light to see by spilled from the house's open doors, Dante scooted back to light a torch and some candles, leaving Lise to tidy the table for something to do. He was companionable enough, but it all felt false somehow. Since their kiss, it had never really left her mind, and she didn't even need to ask if it had gone far from his.

"We ate sandwiches and delicious plantains, and you asked about work, school, and favorite television shows. What's next?" Lise said, watching him half turn toward her, brows raised as she spoke. He had a plan, he had to have a plan.

"Next?"

"I bet if I frisked you, you'd have a list of questions you want to ask hidden somewhere on your body. You have a plan for the evening. It's been more like a job interview and less like a friendly dinner. Am I not getting transferred to your team after all?"

* * *

Dante allowed himself to sit down before answering. She'd been cagey all evening, no matter how polite and civilized he'd made himself behave. "It wasn't a job interview. And I do want to get to know you better."

"I assumed that was code for *I want to get you alone and seduce you*. Other than that, I don't know what your motivation could be for this evening. I'm not that interesting, especially to someone like you."

"Someone like me?" Dante asked. She didn't have the distance sight that could let her unravel him, but he could see her now. It had taken him a little while, but after he figured out that the core of her personality revolved around honesty and gentleness, it hadn't been hard to work his way back to the do-gooder archetype. She didn't trust the rest of flawed humanity, including him right now—which was pretty smart, even if he wasn't going to tell her that.

"You own a nightclub, live in a mansion on a beach, and have people who fly to Florida from far away in order to be treated by you. You're a very different kind of person than I am." She tried to put it all in a positive context, but didn't back away from her usual straightforward manner. He could appreciate that. He could also appreciate that she didn't put herself above him, even if it were true.

Civilized wasn't working because she didn't believe it. She didn't know that much about him, but she knew he was fluid with facts.

"Maybe it's the slickest move in my arsenal: get to know a woman so that I can discern the best way to get her into bed."

He purposefully kept his tone somewhat joking, but held eye contact steady enough to keep her guessing. It would be more fun if she decided to yell at him again anyway.

She stiffened and her hands clasped hard. "That would be an evil thing."

Do-gooder.

"Or just a tool to get the job done."

He leveled his gaze at her over the table, enjoying the golden flicker of the candles and the torch on her face. Over the space of several heartbeats he watched her expression change from shock to consideration. "Is that what you're doing?"

"No." He scooted his chair up and stood, offering her a hand. "But I do have an ulterior motive for the evening."

She eyed his hand, and then purposefully crossed her arms and leaned back in her chair. "Bed, then?"

"Are you offering?"

"No, I'm not offering! I'm asking!" The alarm in her voice was unmistakable, but at least she was displaying emotion now. Emotional Lise was far more entertaining than the reserved and quiet dinner guest.

"I promise to tell you before the evening ends. And I keep my promises." He opened and offered his hand again to her. "I promised you a walk in the surf on a beach not packed with tourists, and it's just over there." Keeping his hand out in invitation, he did step back far enough to keep from crowding her. "That's my main motivation right this second. You and me, walk on the beach."

"You're holding all the power here, but you think I should just pretend everything is okay and walk on the beach because you have an itinerary? What's the plan? First step: dinner. Second step: walk on the beach. Third step: secret seduction?"

"No," he said again, this time sighing. She wasn't going to get off this. Stubborn. "I actually like you. I don't understand how my secrets threaten you. My lust for you has been well documented by this point—so yes, at some point? You and I will end up in bed. Not tonight. But considering how frequently you obliterate my plans, I'm not counting it an impossibility. I've come to understand why you ended up in my club last week."

"Yes. Someone sent me there."

"Not someone. Something bigger. And I want to know more about you before committing."

"Committing? To what?"

"You." He sat back down, frustration taking him. Why did she have to be so difficult? "You were supposed to see me as more than an uptight surgeon, and I was to see that there's more to you than a great, but largely silent nurse."

"That's so silly. You believe that kind of thing?" She shook her head, "That's not how the world works. We have to make our own fate, there's no grand design that grants one person a perfect life and another person a tragic one. So drop that. Just tell me what you want from me. I hate surprises. I hate secrets! Tell me what you want or drive me home right now."

"And there goes another plan," he muttered, half to himself. "I want to marry you. Happy?"

"No, really. What do you want? Be serious."

"Just hear me out. I'm talking about a friends-with-benefits situation, only with rings, and the benefits include procreation."

"Over the last week, since you heard about my plan, you've decided to get married and picked me? I can appreciate that you don't have the same luxury that I have—you can't give birth to your own child—but this is more than a little ridiculous."

"Months ago, getting married became one of my goals. Not a goal I've made any progress on so far—there's no overlap between the eligible women I meet at the club and those I meet at the hospital. And I haven't figured out how to make some kind of dating profile that encompasses both."

"You want to marry me so no one who might tell your stupid secret ends up being your wife?" she shouted at him, then stood up and began stomping toward the beach. "Come on, you wanted a nice romantic walk on the beach, didn't you?" She kicked her sandals off as she stepped down into the sand.

Dante shot out of his chair and caught up with her before she made it five feet off the veranda. "Are you hoping to drown me in the surf?"

"No, you wanted romantic so you could pop the

question, right? Well, it's your lucky day. Might I suggest you continue the cliché by telling me how wonderful I look with the wind in my hair and the freaking moonlight on my face?"

Where had the anger come from? A reflection of his frustration? All he knew was that it amplified the effect. He snatched her closest hand and held on. "Romantic clichéd walks on the beach include hand-holding."

They stomped together, her trying to squirm out of his grasp and him hardening his grip until the water washed up over his feet. Then he stopped. "Tell me what upsets you so much about my secret. It's a nothing secret."

"It's something or it wouldn't be a secret," Lise grunted, and stepped closer to him to stomp on his foot. Hers might be little and without shoes, but she brought it down with enough anger to fill a swimming pool.

He let go of her hand and had to work to keep from grabbing her again.

*Just listen. Let her talk.*

Her talking would give him more information about her, and he really needed that if he was going to have any hope of making this work out right.

"You won't even explain anything to me but you want me to marry you. The only reason you're considering me is to keep me from telling your secret to someone else, and possibly because I'm a professional and have an urgent womb vacancy."

For a moment he had no idea what to say to her. He couldn't even conjure up the right kind of delaying words that would calm her down without giving her too much information.

She stepped back so that there was a good three feet between them, and adopted a pose that let him know exactly how he'd begun to stand: Arms crossed over chest, feet planted as if to withstand attack.

"Let me guess." She laughed the words now, which might be worse. "You're completely stymied because your reputation, your money, and your cold, uninviting beach house were supposed to instantly make me say yes, and then fall into bed for some celebratory sex."

"I'm not stymied."

Yes, he was. Just not for that reason.

The conversation had gotten out of his control the instant she'd planted herself and refused to go amiably along with him to walk on the beach.

There wasn't an accommodating or easy-going bone in her body.

The only thing he knew for sure was that she was easier to talk to when he was touching her.

It might not have been the modern, civilized way to treat a woman, but Dante stepped over to her, grabbed her arm and twirled her into his arms before she could regain her balance. He didn't stop until her back was to his chest and he had his arms around her, her hands clasped in his own.

"What are you doing?"

"You're freaking out," he muttered, "but you're not actually in any danger right now. Calm down."

"Telling someone to calm down never helps them calm down. It only does the reverse. You know that, brain doctor." The words flew out with anger and more than a touch of fear, but she wasn't actually trying to pull free of his arms right now.

Dante would take any advantage he could live with. Of course he had other reasons for choosing her than her womb vacancy and knowledge of the club, but even edging in on those thoughts made him almost as tense as she was, and he really couldn't say them to her out loud. Probably not ever.

He decided not to say anything for the moment.

Just holding her was dampening her initial reaction—which seemed to have been terror expressed as rage and which would definitely need a lighter hand. Hold her, calm her down, maybe actually do some walking, then take her home. Might be the best plan he could put together at this point.

"You wanted to get to know me better before you told me the truth of your motive, so you could decide if I was good enough?"

"No. So I could decide how to best present the proposal. But don't worry about that right now."

"Do you want to get to know me without marriage? Or was this friend thing all part of your marriage scheme?"

"I genuinely want to get to know you. I wouldn't want to marry someone I didn't at least like. I like you, I'm attracted to you. I don't know if love could ever happen between us—my parents set a standard that's impossible for me to live up to. But I want a family. And I'm attracted to you like no other. So I thought…people get married for love and it fails fast all the time. But lust could be a good foundation, as long as it also included friendship. It's like love without all the darker aspects that can get in the way. Jealousy. Possessiveness."

She started to relax in his arms and he felt her anger fade away. She even leaned against him for a moment, then nodded.

Truth? Was truth working? It might have been a modified version—there was definitely more to it than that—but no part of what he'd said had been a lie or orchestrated for a specific result.

"If you want to know me," she said after she finally pulled forward into the surf, and turned to face him. "This is the most important thing you can know about me. I have a very hard time trusting people. You play games, and sometimes I understand that it's fun—it is even probably kind of revealing. If you can get me mad—which you're really good at—then you learn things about me that I might not otherwise offer up to anyone. But this is part of why I can't trust you."

"You can trust me. I wouldn't set out to hurt you."

No. He might set out to make her do something he wanted, but he'd try to minimize the harm that might come to her if he could. If. He. Could.

"I already figured out you have trouble trusting, but I don't know why." He tried to continue on straightforward.

"Secrets. I never know what you're thinking,

and I don't know if that's just because I'm terrible at reading people, or if you're just really good at fooling people. I'm afraid it's that you're really good at fooling people. I know what that looks like in marriage, because that's who my father was."

He already knew her parents were dead—she had no family, the nugget of information that had allowed him to envision a mutually beneficial situation between them.

"When did your parents die?" he asked, and tugged her hands a little so that she stepped forward enough that their arms weren't stretched to the limit between one another. Closer was better for these kinds of conversations. Sad stories were hard enough to share when you didn't have to shout them over the roar of the ocean.

He watched her face go from pensive and pink from the remains of their red-faced argument to pale grief in an instant. He might've been able to distance himself enough from the telling of the story to do it calmly, but she couldn't.

"Was it recently?"

She shook her head and lowered her gaze, first to his shoulders then his chest, then off to the side of him. "My father shot himself in the head when I was eleven, after lying to everyone for years. His business was in a shambles, afloat because of unethical business practices and over-extended credit."

He wanted her to look him in the eye. The past week he'd spent his time thinking that her devotion to unwavering honesty was quaint and sweet, but could see that it came from a much darker place now. Nothing but looking her in the eye would allow him to see how much.

Her hands still in his, he stepped in again until they were inches apart, and lifted her hands to his chest to rest against him. It made her look up at him, and when he let go of her hands to put his arms around her, she left them there.

Shot in the head. There was a rawness in her eyes that let him know she'd seen it.

Redirect. Help her gain a little distance. "He killed himself over a failing business?"

"That was part of it. He also genuinely loved my mother, I think. But he'd started self-medicating his business worries with alcohol, stopped spending time at home, and she sought affection from another man. Men, actually. There were a couple. He found out, they fought about it, and after she went to bed he shot himself in the downstairs study."

Downstairs study. She'd been born to privilege, even if it was a kind of fake privilege, wool pulled over their eyes.

He should stop asking her for details, but now that she was actually letting him see her, letting him inside, he couldn't stop. It would be worse if he made her go through this twice in order to find out how to convince her to marry him. "Who found him?"

"We both found him. We heard the shot. We both got up, she stopped me at the stairs and told me to go hide, but my dad hadn't come running from the room with her. I knew he wasn't upstairs, and it was so late that he had to be in the house." And the horror had never left her. "I waited for her to make it down the stairs before giving in and tearing after her. I got to the office while she was still screaming."

It was in him to ask her about the gun, to know exactly how graphic a death it had been, but that look in her eyes told him what he needed to know. Small-caliber bullets could kill as effectively as shotguns, but big guns left the most horrific scenes, and they left a mark on anyone who saw them. His own father had survived a small-caliber shot to the head for hours before he died, but he'd only had a small hole in his head, he'd still looked normal but for that small red hole. But a shotgun…

Don't make her say it. He closed his arms until she stepped in enough to rest her cheek on his shoulder, her arms folded against his chest, not hugging back but accepting the comfort he offered.

Change the subject. "How did your mom pass away?"

Losing both his parents at the same time had been horrible, but having two tragic traumatic death memories to deal with? It was too much. He could only pray because he couldn't actually hold her any closer.

The wound he dug at helped him understand her and her aversion to secrets, but there was nothing here he could fix.

"Heart attack. It was quick."

"And sudden?" Still tragic, but less devastating.

"Not really. She'd been feeling unwell for a while, but wouldn't go to the doctor. And she smoked like a chimney. One morning she got up, and the rapid increase of blood pressure triggered a heart attack."

"Did you find her too?"

Still tucked against him, she shook her head. "She called 911 but died before they reached her. I was at school and the police came to tell me. I didn't have to find her. Her death was easier, and I'd learned very well how to adapt by then. Dropped out of the nursing program, signed up for the short surgical tech program, and after getting a job with that I went back to my RN program."

She'd learned to adapt because even from a very young age her family had let her down. He'd had a hard path, but he'd never truly walked it alone.

"I'm not like your father," he said suddenly, sliding his hands to her shoulders so he could push her back just far enough to look him in the eye. In that instant he knew that was the biggest obstacle to his proposal, and he needed her to understand the difference.

This wasn't something he could charm his way past, it was a real, honest part of who she was—it came from too dark a place to be a noble whim.

"Lies and secrets." She whispered the words, and the ocean stole the sound from him, but he saw the words on her lips.

He shook his head. "It's not the same."

"Lies are lies."

This particular subject required the respect of honesty. Even if she claimed to never know when he was lying, she still responded as if she knew. That was enough.

"I understand why he lied to you and your mother about his failing business. He thought he was protecting you from it. But what I don't understand is why he didn't do anything to fix the situation, and I don't understand how he could abandon you both. I would never do that."

"It's easy to say that."

"I haven't always been an upstanding citizen. Okay? When we were trying to stay together—not let Alejandro and Santi go into the system—I learned that double life that you hate. We needed money and I brought it in however I had to. I did things that I will...should forever be ashamed of. But I did them because I was taking care of people I loved and who depended on me. That's how we're different."

"They let you do immoral things?"

"They didn't know. I could always come up with a story. That's what it is to be a man: you take care of your family. My father was dead, and our family needed someone to step up. Rafe stepped up too, just differently." He didn't want to get off on that tangent—she didn't need to know all those illegal and immoral things he'd done in the name of taking care of his loved ones, she just had to understand that he was only like her father at a glance. "I understand that your family let you down from the very beginning. That's not the Valentino way."

Lise stepped away from him. He could've hauled her back against him, kept her there, with the fruity fragrant scent of her hair blending in with his every breath, but he couldn't force his way through this.

She looked him full in the eye, and though she looked a little worried now, at least she didn't look defeated anymore.

"Please don't get mad," she said, hand up in front of her, so wary of him minutes after she'd nuzzled into him like she needed him, like she trusted him.

"I won't get mad." He said the words she needed and waited, letting his arms fall lax at his sides.

"I know you mean that in the best possible way, but it places you above your brothers. It assumes that they need protecting from things still."

"They don't need to carry the weight of my sins, that's why I don't tell them now."

"The club is a sin?"

"The club…" He didn't want to get into that, the night had already been heavy enough. "It's tied to my old ways."

"Are you in the Mafia or something?" she asked suddenly, and Dante almost laughed.

"I am not now, nor have I ever been affiliated with organized crime. If anything, I was the organized one. Occasionally, someone from my past looks me up at The Inferno. I try my best to keep those people from circles where it could get back to my family. All that is beside the point. The point is this: whether or not you agree with my reasons for not being open about everything, you have to acknowledge that I don't do it to hurt the people I love."

"That's true. I can accept that you think that you have to protect them—even if they're grown men—but you have to acknowledge that you'll do the same thing with your wife. Even if I was willing to take that kind of a risk on someone to get married, I couldn't take it with you."

"You already walk equally well with me in both worlds. You're unique but also interesting. My family would like you." He could feel the thread of this slipping away from him.

"Still, you're not talking about dating, you're going straight from one dinner to the altar!"

"I'm not suggesting that you immediately fall in love with me. You're rushing headlong into pregnancy, can you fault me for acknowledging there's a ticking clock on this? You're not onboard yet, but I'm certain. We get along very well, and we have more chemistry than I've ever felt with anyone. We also have a common goal: to have a family, raise good kids, have a nice, safe life."

One hand lifted and she rubbed at her forehead, then paced past him, then around, and as she spun he realized she was circling, moving to move, and if he kept following her, it might end in his first case of motion sickness ever, and very possibly the world's worst proposal ending: vomiting on her wouldn't help her come round.

He planted his feet and waited for her to come around again.

"I understand, but it's too much too soon."

"Are you willing to delay getting pregnant to give it a chance?"

"I don't know, Dante. My first instinct is to say no. If you can't understand that after all that I told you, my instinct is right." She stopped in front of him and let her eyes connect with his. "If it makes you feel better, I haven't picked the donor I want yet. I couldn't even tell you what delaying would be since I haven't got a set schedule."

That was something to wrest from this evening.

She'd upset all his plans. Would she even if he planned, then planned the exact thing in reverse?

With one hand, she gestured behind them at the house—they had ostensibly gone to the beach to have a walk, but they'd taken root at the shore-line and proceeded to argue and open old wounds with one another.

"I'm tired. Really tired. I need to go home."

# CHAPTER SIX

LISE MADE A conscious decision to go into work somewhat later than her usual half an hour early, precisely because she didn't want to be cornered by Dante—which she really didn't think he'd do soon, but if they were alone, she'd see the question in his eyes. And the only answer she had for him wouldn't please him at all. That was, if she could even get him to accept rejection.

The truth was, shutting down the idea entirely was equal parts relief and a kind of stomach-plummeting queasy feeling. She knew it wasn't the right decision to say yes—there was no way for her to trust him right now, no matter how convincing he'd been at explaining the difference between his and her father's secrets. She couldn't say yes until she could tell whether or not he was for real or if he was just playing with her.

Even with the untrustworthy issues, she wished she could just say yes. He'd put his arms around her and talked her through the worst night of her life, and she'd felt safe. When they'd been fighting and stomping around on the beach, she'd still felt mostly safe. Or at least physically safe. It was the emotional safety that she couldn't reconcile. He could be hiding who he really was. People hid the bad parts of themselves and she couldn't spot a good liar.

And she couldn't decide if her and her mother's lives would've been better if her father had never been with them. There had been no recovering after that, it had just been getting through each day, learning to survive. She needed security for her future babies, even if she could weather a lot on her own now.

Tugging the hem of her new scrub top straight, she rushed into the scrub bay off the morning's scheduled OR. As with every week, she'd be in surgery with Dante on Monday and Thursday, with her midweek spent with other surgeons. So she'd have a little time to come up with a way to say no to him and to give it enough time that it looked like she'd given the request the serious consideration it deserved. It hadn't been easy for him to ask, and it wouldn't be easy to say no.

He'd said he liked her, and she definitely liked

him, almost as much as she regularly wanted to stomp on his toes.

When she stepped in, Dante was still at the scrub bay, but he turned and immediately met her gaze, stopping all movement where he'd been busily working his fingernails over with a scrub brush.

She smiled, tried to feign normalcy—whatever that was. "Good morning, Dr. Valentino."

"Bradshaw," he returned, as calm and focused in the OR as ever. She still had time to handle this. "We've had a change in patient and procedure this morning."

"How did that happen? What are we doing?"

"We're going to try and stabilize an aneurysm in a patient who came in through the ER early this morning, and then the plan is to bring our scheduled non-emergency patient in directly after."

She grabbed a brush, unwrapped it and stepped to the sink to start scrubbing in, while trying to ignore the man at her side. Impossible task. Every inch of her body seemed to go on high alert when she was near him and it didn't even go away when they fought. When he looked at her, she felt it, no matter how fleeting a glance.

Dante waited for the room to clear except for

them before focusing on her. "It's going to be a long day, and since you're assisting me, it'll put more stress on you than the rest of the team. If you get to where you feel you're not giving your best, I want you to tell me. We'll swap someone in for you."

"You doubt my endurance?" Lise asked, tilting her head at him.

"Everyone gets tired sometimes. Especially if they're mentally preoccupied with something else."

"I'm not going to be preoccupied, Doctor, but to put your mind at ease—" because she *could* put his mind at ease about this, if nothing else "—that's how I'd always work. My ego wouldn't prevent me from telling you if I wasn't able to give my best. You have my word on that."

He looked at her a little longer than was necessary, but nodded. "I appreciate being put at ease. It's always a good thing."

There it was, the first allusion to their personal situation. But, ever the professional, that's all he said about it, and then he was heading for the operating room.

Letting things drag out until she felt comfortable was selfish and unkind. After surgery, she should tell him, give him a chance to cancel her transfer if he wanted. Maybe she should even encourage it. They'd have the whole rest of the week to find some way to be around one another normally.

Shame that he wouldn't want to get to know her further after she made her "no" official. It was nice to be with him, even when they were arguing.

Within half an hour, their patient was under general anesthesia and Dante had begun, his attention entirely on what he was doing, and Lise worked on smoothness of delivery and anticipation of his needs while others observed the patient's vitals, kept him under and in no pain.

Lise shook her head minutely and took the scalpel back from Dante, who'd moved on to a bone saw that would allow him to begin the small craniotomy behind the patient's right temple, above the ear, to gain access to the blood vessel he needed to track into the brain so he could stop the bleeding.

Don't think about the talk they were going to have.

Another day and she still hadn't told him.

It seemed to Lise that her life changed dramatically in between all her Dante surgery days anyway. If that pace kept up after she'd been transferred and had consecutive Dante days in a row, she might lose her mind.

Not that her hold on sanity was especially strong after this weekend anyway, without even considering the prospect that every day could be Monday and she might end up dithering outside the doors leading into the surgical suite, trying to steel her resolve to see him and discover how her body would react that day.

In the beginning, she'd thought it was just a sexual reaction to him, an entirely physical pull, but the more she saw him, the more it became something else. She could feel him in the air before he appeared. Their everyday interaction had begun to change too—sometimes he looked at her with that devastating look of desire, and other looks felt different, but she couldn't quite name them.

His badly-planned proposal had changed things between them because of how angry she'd gotten. She knew him better now, she thought. She hoped... But she knew that he knew her better also. Was this the kind of time that people put in to get to know one another so they could become close? She'd always started with common interests in the past.

Maybe both of them wanting a family and children was their common interest.

Or maybe he kept coming around because he could understand that part of her past she usually did her best not to think about. No one else in Miami knew about her father.

Someone would find them out before long if they didn't figure out a way to make their work relationship function. If that was even possible now. Dante could pull it off better than she could. He was so used to keeping secrets that there was no way he'd be the one to crack and say the wrong thing in front of the others.

It was *her*. She was the problem. She was the one who'd spent the weekend alternating between giving herself hell and giving herself pep talks—both for allowing herself to become the woman she was, and for her certainty that her self-protective measures had done precisely what she'd needed: kept her safe by keeping dangers at a distance.

What she couldn't accept was that by her current practices everyone was a danger to her. The loneliness had to end.

Time for another pep talk.

Transferring to his team would blow up in both

their faces. She had to put a stop to it now, before the week ended—just as she'd kept telling herself for the last week. Yes, neurosurgery was her favorite, but there was something to be said for not specializing—her usual nursing skills wouldn't get rusty or abandon her if she didn't stop using them entirely by specializing.

He was nearby. She knew it like she knew the way her body always reacted to his proximity, like something touched her.

A quick tuck to make certain all flyaway strands of her hair had been contained under her cap, and Lise opened the door.

"I was wondering if you were going to go in," Dante said from directly behind her. She paused and looked back at him, that alone probably confirming all the conflicting thoughts zooming through her mind.

She may've been a little too absorbed to have immediately noticed today, and she'd blame him for keeping her too wound up to function properly.

He reached past her and grabbed the door to take over holding it open, his proximity letting her momentarily banish the hospital's usual stringent odors and flood her sinuses with his special brand of spicy, distracting warmth.

"Go on," he said, his voice whisper-soft, certain not to carry, even down the empty halls where all sounds found echoes. "The OR is sacrosanct."

Something she knew but had momentarily forgotten: Dante didn't take chances with his patients. Or his family, by the sound of things.

But that one statement made clear to her that outside the OR he wasn't done with her.

Needing space, she made herself nod and then hurried to the furthest scrub sink, fully expecting him to follow despite his declaration.

He didn't. And that was a good thing.

She'd be glued to his side for the next few hours anyway—but these little scrub-sink chats weren't helping her think clearly. The only reason—aside from her feckless attraction to him—she couldn't keep temptation at bay was how much she looked forward to seeing him, talking to him. So far, all conversation with others failed to move her to feel anything.

The vigor with which he protected his family added to his draw. If it were true… But that was impossible to determine without tracking down a sibling and spilling his secrets.

She had to work this out on her own.

Especially if she was to have any hope of continuing to ignore how much she wanted to throw caution to the wind and at least have one night with him, like a consolation prize to the proposal she could not accept.

"Surgery's cancelled," Sandy said as soon as Lise entered the surgical suite early Thursday morning, the last day that she'd be assigned to the unit.

"Why?" she asked, stepping up to help Sandy strip down the prep work she'd already done to get the OR ready for their early morning patient.

Marisol came in, and Sandy repeated herself, then answered Lise with a teasing grin, "No one told me that. You could ask Dr. Valentino."

"Why would I ask him?" Lise asked, and only realized after it came out that her tone sounded guilty. People had been picking up on the tension between them after all, it seemed. And she'd thought they'd done such a good job of keeping under the radar.

Sandy looked at her oddly over the table. "Because you're transferring to his team Monday?"

"Oh..." She breathed the word, looking between the two women who were now both openly staring at her. The weight of their stares made it clear to Lise just how badly she'd just given them away.

People with nothing to hide didn't get defensive over unimportant things.

"You sure you don't want me to stay and help you get this back in order first?"

It wasn't a delaying tactic. Though she really could use some lessons in how to use those.

"Pretty sure. If we don't have surgery this morning, I've got some errands to catch up on," Sandy said.

"And I have continuing education courses to finish before tomorrow."

Both of them wanted to leave. He was her new boss starting Monday. This was what came from dragging one's feet on decision-making—prior decisions got to roll out.

She just hadn't been able to commit to stopping the transfer—it had felt like shutting down all their business, and she couldn't bring herself to do that no matter how many pep talks she gave herself.

Employing her fastest nurse walk, Lise made it to Dante's office before she'd even let herself consider much beyond the realization that she'd not spent any time alone with him since that night on the beach.

She'd just reached for the doorknob when the door blew open and Dante slammed right into her.

Dante jerked back into focus on his path to Emergency, specifically onto Lise stumbling back from him, tilted off her axis.

He grabbed her shoulders to steady her, and even with the buzz of an emergency in the air, his body reacted to merely touching her. Nothing overt, but his pulse bumped up another notch, and his hands tingled.

"What's wrong?" she blurted out, her hands wrapping around his wrists as she steadied herself.

"Emergency just called. We've got a bad head trauma coming in. Call the others, tell them to prep the OR as soon as possible." He let go of her and stepped back, the motion causing her to let go of his arms too. "And then come down with me. West ambulance bay."

She fumbled for the in-hospital com system all medical personnel carried.

"Come on, Bradshaw. Walk and talk at the same time," he shouted over his shoulder as he reached the stairwell.

The ambulance had been three minutes out when they'd called in to the ED, and he'd been called immediately after. He might still be able to meet the ambulance if he hurried.

He jogged through the west receiving bay just as the ambulance pulled in, the only physician there to meet them.

When it stopped rolling, he rounded to the back and wrenched the doors open. The sound of a wailing baby was the first thing that reached him. Scanning the dim interior of the ambulance, he made out the stretcher with an immobilized and unconscious patient, a paramedic, and a red-faced, harried police officer holding a baby just short of a year, and soaked in blood.

"Is he injured?" Dante asked the paramedic, but moved back so they could remove the stretcher.

"We didn't find any injuries on him, but he was unconscious at the scene. Doubt he fell asleep in his car seat, most likely knocked out, but was still strapped in. He woke when they began cutting into the car to get to him and his mother." The paramedic gestured to the unconscious mother, whose head was covered in bloody bandages. Even with the bulk from the makeshift dressing, Dante could tell that along the crown of her forehead, her skull dented in a devastating fashion.

Dante took the child, who wasn't affixed to

the stretcher and didn't have any first-aid apparatuses attached to him. His one-piece, blue-and-white-striped romper had far too much dark-red blood saturating it. The cheerful-faced puppy on the front seemed to have absorbed the most blood, and stuck the material to his tiny chest.

One look back confirmed that Lise had caught up with him. She looked so stricken that his wheels started spinning. Opportunity... He immediately held the baby out to her.

"Take him inside. You're off this surgery—I want you to stay with him. I'm sure the ED nurses can handle things, but he lost consciousness, and I'd prefer a nurse from Neuro keeping a sharp eye on him," he said, as she wrapped the baby in her arms, clutching him protectively to her chest, and Dante knew his instinct had been right. It'd do her good to have a living reminder of how helpless babies and small children were, especially when something happened to a parent and they were beholden to the kindness of strangers until family could retrieve them.

They'd wheeled the mother into the hospital, so he put a hand on Lise's shoulder and steered her inside. The baby continued to scream, so he spoke loudly over him. "What are you looking for? Symptoms."

Lise cuddled the baby close and added a little extra bounce to her step as they hurried down the hallway. *What symptoms?* It took a moment for her to summon them. "Ah, loss of consciousness, confusion, vomiting, irregular pupil reaction..."

"Right. Stay with him until they either transfer him to Children's Hospital or he's given to family. And send someone into my OR to alert me if anything changes."

"What about your surgery?"

The look he gave her said everything. The mother wasn't going to survive, and he knew it already, but he was still going in. He had to try... but the baby was still his top priority.

"Okay," she said, and met a nurse hurrying toward them.

His little body stayed stiff in her arms, his breathing ragged and uneven as he continued to scream himself out of breath.

The room she was led to had a crib and specialist equipment. This was why she couldn't work in Emergency full time. She could handle it when things happened to adults—accidents, violence, and illness—but she'd never cared for an injured or ill child without crying, though never in front of them, but after her shift it could wipe her out.

"I'll get him something else to wear, a fresh diaper, and a wash pan. We need to get that blood off him. That might calm him down some," the other nurse said, unflappable with the whole situation—or at least able to keep from showing it.

The instructions made sense but would require her putting him down, and something primitive and horrified screamed inside Lise. *Don't put him down. Don't let him go.*

But holding him wasn't helping right now. Cleaning him up might.

She laid him carefully in the crib and quickly stripped the sodden clothing off his tiny body.

For being so small, he kicked and tried to roll, frantic and fighting in the mindless way of an angry, traumatized baby.

"It's okay," she said on autopilot, not that he was likely to understand in his current state. His name. She didn't know his name.

Talking didn't work, but she caught him and got him on his back long enough to unfasten the diaper before he tried to roll again. Still. Screaming.

Every cry bit into her. Her stomach rolled and she clenched her jaw, trying to control the visceral reaction she had to the pain she heard wringing out of him, while also trying to do whatever he needed.

The nurse came back with supplies and Lise asked her, "Do you know his name?"

"No one knows it yet."

Lise focused on the other nurse's badge and said, "Ginny, can you bring the water here? I don't want to take him to the sink. He's surprisingly strong, and when wet..."

"Right." A moment later, a tray had been rolled to the crib and Lise held him while Ginny spread an absorbent pad on the mattress and began washing away the blood, first from his face and matted hair, and then down over his chest.

His mother had lost so much blood. How could she still be alive?

They switched off when he got slippery and started gaining ground on them. Ginny lifted him by the armpits until he dangled; it was the only way to keep his feet out of play at times.

In short order, his dark skin had been washed completely clean, but once he was on a fresh towel and Lise was drying him, she noticed marks. "He's got a matching set of bruises forming on top of his shoulders." Then described the position better, so Ginny could chart it.

"You know, I appreciate your help with him—that was definitely a two-person job—but if you want to return to Neurology, I can take him." Everything they said had to be projected from the diaphragm to be heard over his angry, still terrified cries.

"Dr. Valentino ordered me to stay with him," Lise said, even though she felt a little strange saying it. "He wants a nurse from Neuro doing constant checks for signs of head trauma—concussion, bleeding, things that can happen from sudden violent movements."

Shaken-baby-syndrome-style bleeding could be caused by an accident as well as by a monstrous person.

Lise finished drying him and began the process of wrestling him into a fresh diaper and a tiny hospital gown.

"Give me your ID," Ginny said, "or give him to me and run to get yourself another scrub top from the machine."

Lise looked down and saw it then: the mom's blood had soaked into her top from the baby's saturated romper. She had to change, but even if

Dante hadn't told her to stay, her whole body reacted to the idea of leaving him.

Pulling her ID off, she handed it to Ginny, rattled off her sizes—yes, an XL top—and added her sincere thanks before tying the towel over her so she could pick him up in the meantime. At least that way, he couldn't kick himself out of the crib, and it made her feel like she was at least giving him some comfort, though no one could tell it from the way he cried.

A few minutes later, Ginny returned with the new top, and held the baby while Lise changed into the familiar tent-like scrub tops she used to wear, and then she had him held against her again, and rocked and shushed him softly as she walked around the cubicle.

When there was a screaming, inconsolable baby in the department, the doctors came fast. "His name is Elijah," a woman in turquoise scrubs and a white lab jacket announced as she stepped into the room. "I'm Dr. Arushi Dhawan—haven't you been able to calm him?"

"No," Lise admitted. "I don't know if he understands that his mommy is hurt, or if he's still reacting to the terror that no doubt came over him from the accident, or just being surrounded by strangers now..."

Dr. Dhawan ordered a mild sedative, and Lise couldn't argue against it. Examining him would be all but impossible with him in this state.

Ten minutes later, the screaming stopped and the doctor could listen to the baby's breathing and heart, palpate for any actual physical pains or hardness in his abdomen, and check pupillary reaction.

"I think he's been badly jostled, but he seems physically okay. I'd rather not expose him to imaging without a good reason. You're staying with him, correct?"

"Yes."

"And you are with Dr. Valentino's team?"

"Yes."

"Okay, so you know how to check his pupillary reactions, yes?"

Lise confirmed this as well.

"Check every ten minutes. He'll probably start to come out of the sedation in half an hour or so, but if you're lucky he may stay asleep longer. Get Ginny to order some food, bottle, whatever you need, and try to keep him calm. If you note anything concerning, you can call me directly: Arushi Dhawan. Okay?"

Lise lifted the baby back out of the crib just to hold him, and once more confirmed the instructions. "Thank you, Doctor. Do you know how they found out his name?"

"Someone from the mother's workplace recognized the car on the highway and called the police to check after she got to work."

"Does he have family coming for him? His father?"

"That I don't know, but I hope so." Dr. Dhawan repeated the instructions, and then slipped out.

"I hope your daddy comes, Elijah. Eli. I think it's Eli..." She pulled her flashlight from her pocket and got ready to check his pupils.

He'd sleep through this while the sedative was still in his system, but she harbored no hope that he'd sleep through the neuro checks she'd keep doing after it wore off. She'd take an inconsolable infant over one that quietly slipped away because his nurse didn't want to wake him.

She would still hope they'd find his daddy soon.

# CHAPTER SEVEN

By two in the afternoon, Lise had settled into Eli's hospital room. He'd been admitted for overnight observation, and none of his family had yet materialized for him. She couldn't leave.

He went through periods now and then when his volume decreased, and it seemed like he might be calming down, but the faintest noise would set him off again.

Every half hour she tried to get him to eat something or take a bottle.

Milk, refused. Apple juice, refused. She even tried chocolate milk, and he didn't want that either.

Nearing midnight, long after she'd begun needing to swipe her cheeks before the unit nurses came to check on him, lying back in a stiff leather recliner, Eli finally gave in to exhaustion and fell asleep on her chest.

Afraid to wake him, she simply lay with him,

holding on, giving whatever comfort his tiny, bruised body and soul would accept in slumber.

A couple of hours later at shift change, the new RN came to check on him and informed Lise that an aunt had been located in Tennessee and was expected to arrive in the morning.

In the silence as she waited out the night, one encompassing fear ricocheted through her.

What if he'd had no family to come for him?

What if Dante hadn't wanted a neurological nurse to stay with him?

What if he'd been her child?

Would there have been someone to hold him while he sobbed and screamed his way through the trauma?

Lise knocked hard on Dante's front door. She'd rung the bell twice already, maybe her knuckles would resound through the beach house enough to get him to the door.

Even if she looked like death, Lise couldn't bring herself to care. She needed to see him.

She waited. It felt like hours, but probably wasn't even a whole minute.

What could be taking so long?

Giving in to compulsion, she mashed the door-bell a third time.

No patience left, she hopped off his front porch and barreled around the large house to the veranda, praying those doors were open.

He was probably sleeping in. Sleeping!

Without even checking once to see how Eli was doing after handing the bloody baby off to her about twenty-five hours ago. She wanted to smack Dante and then wrap his arms around her so she could get that feeling again—like he'd held her that night on the beach.

Ducking around the breakfast table, she made it to the French doors and tried the knobs.

Locked. Every part of her ached—body, heart, mind—and he couldn't even answer the door.

She knocked again and yelled his name this time.

Was he drunk in there?

Dead?

In bed with someone he'd picked up at the club last night?

This was stupid.

Energy depleted, she spun away from the doors. Spotting a large, closed beach umbrella leaning against the house, she grabbed it, opened it, and stepped off the veranda to bring the handle down into the sand with all her might. She'd wait, but she'd do it in shade. It had been too hard a night to sit here and burn up—the sun was already higher than the horizon and it was August.

She'd just bent to sit on the step when she heard the French doors open.

"Lise? For God's sake, stay at one door until someone—"

Lise heard his voice and turned to look back at the doors she'd been rattling. Dante stood there in the open door, wearing nothing but boxers.

Dante struggled to see in the bright sunshine at his back door. When sleepy eyes adjusted, irritation died in his throat.

Crying. She'd been crying. And she was wearing her old scrubs—but this was Friday, and they didn't work Fridays.

"She died?" The question came from her as a cry. "When you operated? She died? What happened?"

She was still awake from yesterday? The realization settled in his gut like lead.

"Did you have the baby all night?"

"Yes. His aunt drove down from Nashville and

came straight to the hospital, got there an hour ago." Her lower lip quivered while she spoke. "He wouldn't stop crying. He wouldn't eat or drink anything. They had to sedate him to examine him, he couldn't stop crying!"

Her eyes grew rounder and rounder as she spoke, tears stood in her eyes and she blinked rapidly to try and dispel it.

Even without a drop of food in his stomach, Dante could've vomited. What had he been thinking?

Opportunity had presented itself, a way to subtly urge Lise to come around to his way of thinking, reinforce the idea that it would be valuable for her children to have a father, not just a sperm donor. A way to recommend himself without saying another word.

And he hadn't hesitated, even though it had involved exploiting something personal about her past that hurt her, that shined a light on the fact that she had no family.

It should've been two or three hours max, not twenty-four. Not a night of emotional torture.

Still only in his boxers, Dante made a direct line for her across the veranda and pulled her against him.

"She died?" she croaked against his chest, like she couldn't quite believe it. He should have words for her but his throat refused to work, to make words. So he nodded against her head and cleared his throat. This was it, something he'd hoped would never happen: fresh, potent shame—one of two things he could feel guilty over.

After a night like that she deserved an answer.

He tried again. "She died on the table. We were there nearly twelve hours, trying to get her skull back together and remove glass and splintered bone from where the debris was cutting in. I don't know how she lasted that long. I'm sorry. I'm so sorry, Lise. I didn't think you'd still be with him at that time, and Dr. Dhawan told me he'd had no neurological symptoms. So I left."

He felt her tears wetting his bare chest, squeezed her tighter, and steered her back into the house.

She was crying.

*Dios!*

The sofa was the closest thing to sit her down on, but it should've been like her sofa. What comfort could be gotten from this hard leather thing?

Still, he sat with her, tugging her back against him.

No more words came that might help. He could

engineer an experience designed to play on her weaknesses and manipulate her into doing what he wanted, but he couldn't think of a single thing that would make it better afterward.

In silence they sat, the soft sniffling now in the crook of his neck gutting him over and over.

"Tell me," he finally said when her tears didn't seem near to stopping. "Tell me everything that happened."

*So I can fix it.*

She looked up at him, eyes red and swollen, and it all began to tumble out. Her heartbreak for little Eli. How she'd prayed for his mother the whole night as she'd sat holding him, afraid to move because he'd finally fallen asleep. The relief she'd felt when Aunt Nikki had arrived and he'd finally taken a bottle and eaten some oatmeal.

The crush of guilt that had bloomed in her when—while Aunt Nikki had fed and held Eli so he could feel her presence—Lise had asked for an update on the mother and found out that she'd died.

Guilt wasn't a strong enough word for that kind of mistake. Apologies tumbled from her lips again and he knew she wasn't apologizing to him.

Nothing could make this better for them.

Every part of the account pummeled him, a series of body blows. By the time she'd purged the hours of sadness, frustration, pity and fear, all he could do was what she'd tried to do for that baby. Hold her. Offer his pathetic, useless wish for her comfort.

Heedless of his inappropriate state of dress, he pulled her into his lap and kissed her face, then wound the wet, salty kisses to her mouth.

Like lightning hitting dried wood, the spark erupted and Lise caught his face, holding his mouth to hers. No sweet, badly aimed smooch this time. She leaned into it, hungry, starved, and bleeding need into the blistering kiss. An ache exploded in him like he'd never experienced, summoning his own guilt back to the front, into that part of his brain housing his often neglected conscience.

Her salt-tinged kisses stung.

*"No. No puedo, ángel..."*

"Please." She spoke English, making him realize that he'd slipped into Spanish on her.

"I can't. Not right now."

"But that's what I need. Please?"

In that moment he couldn't tell what would make him less of a bastard—giving her the comfort she wanted or refusing to because she was too vulnerable to really comprehend it.

Another look into her eyes, and he got his answer. Her need wasn't for sex. It was for solace.

"Come to bed. We'll sleep." He stroked her hair back, but kept one arm anchored around her shoulders to keep her close. "You're exhausted. You can curl up with me. It'll be better after you sleep."

"You don't want me right now?" she asked, then added, "Too snotty?"

He smiled at that, but only to recognize the hint of humor he still saw in her through the heartache.

"Too heartbroken for you and that baby," he whispered.

And too heartbroken over what he'd done.

His words seemed to resonate with her. She sniffed, rubbed her bleary eyes, and climbed off his lap. "Okay, but don't let go of me."

"I promise."

The bedroom wasn't far, and he steered her there after a stop to lock up the veranda doors.

The bed he'd just crawled out of would still be warm, and now that the tears had stopped she looked like she could collapse at any second, like the only thing keeping her upright was stress.

He sat her on the edge, then knelt down to get her shoes off, then lifted her feet to encourage her into the bed in her scrubs.

Planting her hands on the mattress, she shifted her feet from his grasp. "No."

"You don't want to sleep?"

In answer, she leaned on her elbows and lifted her bottom, tugging the scrub bottoms down to her thighs. The will to complete the task left her, or maybe her strength just failed. She flopped onto her back and lifted her knees to him. "Can you?"

Help her get comfortable.

Dante tried not to stare, not to ogle her, not to let that spark of desire in them flare back up. He was supposed to be comforting her, undoing the damage he'd done. This wasn't him pulling the clothes off his lover, not yet. Even if he wasn't looking now, his mind kept replaying the glimpse he'd allowed himself of the clingy pink panties encasing her curves and the way the color complemented her pale skin.

Not the time for those thoughts.

*Solace. Not sex.*

Once he slid the bottoms down, she lifted her hands to him and he helped her sit back up.

Before he could ease her back into the bed, she released his hands and whisked the scrub top off as well and tossed it onto the floor.

If he knew one thing about women, he knew that bra was coming off next.

His intentions right now were good but shaky. If he stayed standing there, letting her disrobe before his eyes...

He wasn't strong enough for that.

Leaning onto the bed beside her, he levered himself up to the top of the bed so that the sight of delightfully large breasts he'd glimpsed encased in the matching pink bra couldn't tear down his composure or his resistance. The view of her back was temptation enough... The dip of her waist... The flare of her hips.

"Do you want a T-shirt or something?"

"No." She reached behind her and slid up the bed toward him and his flagging restraint, every inch making heavy dents in his limping morality.

"Lise, we're going to sleep."

She half turned toward him, baring those glorious breasts to him and completely derailing his thought process.

"I want skin," she said, her voice soft and tired.

"I need to feel skin. It could be your back. I just need contact."

The weariness in her voice was enough to tear his gaze away from the curves upon curves.

Lying back, he opened his arms and she crawled into them, settling her body at his side and tucking her face against his neck.

Through the guilt, and even through the sexual fog that dampened his ability to think—in the back of his mind he still felt it—that exultant preen that wanted to crow his victory.

He tamped it down but couldn't fail to acknowledge he'd won. She'd marry him now.

She'd say yes, and he'd figure out some way to make this right.

Later.

After she slept enough to stop trembling.

The last remnants of light faded the twilight sky to dark blue, and Dante looked back down at Lise sleeping on his chest. She lay sprawled, facedown across him, her cheek pressed into his shoulder, face turned up so he'd been able to spend the last hour studying her face in sleep as the light faded from the room.

Peaceful, so peaceful he'd delayed waking her,

even though her stomach had been growling intermittently for at least as long as he'd been awake.

He didn't even want to know how long she'd gone without eating because of him, but somehow doubted that she'd eaten anything while in the hospital, trying to take care of the inconsolable baby, and he knew she hadn't since he'd been trying to take care of an inconsolable Lise.

And he'd be further damned if she got through to another calendar day without eating on his watch.

Carefully, wanting her to sleep until the last possible minute, he plucked his phone from the bedside table, and in a few clicks had a pizza ordered for delivery.

An hour later, after the doorbell rang through the house without waking her, he made his stealthy trip to the door. Dropping the delivery on a table in the living room, he made his way back to her, eased into the bed and touched her arm. "Wake up, Sleeping Beauty."

Light shone through the open door, letting him see the instant consciousness returned to her. Lise's pale blue eyes peeked open, and she stretched hard, then scooted closer to him. "You smell like pizza."

"It's my new cologne." He smiled at her sleepy face, doing his best to be gentle with her and not let his libido steer this conversation. He had to get her out of this bed if he was going to get a line on how she was doing before he complicated things.

He eased off the bed and moved toward the door. "Get up, then. I put some clothes on the bureau for you."

It felt good just taking care of her. It was the second time he'd felt compelled to do that, and neither time had been as altruistic as it would've been had she been the one doing the caring.

"I don't want to get up."

Dante stopped at the door and turned back to look at her. The light spilling into the dark room was like a spotlight—her pale skin glowed, and there was a lot to see. She'd sat up, and the sheet pooled around her waist. The breasts he'd been strenuously avoiding actually seeing stood proudly from her slender shoulders. Everything he'd been imagining since he'd seen her in that red dress.

His neck started to sweat. He had to drag his gaze away before his body responded.

"You have to eat something." It all came out a little rougher than he wanted, but it felt like every word was a struggle even to take shape in his mind.

When he looked at her again he realized he'd somehow moved all the way back to the bed, only stopping when the beaded edge of the mattress pressed into his shin.

"No."

With the grunt of an old man standing from too comfortable a chair, Dante tried to right the course of his thoughts—which were going right where she was leading. Back to bed. On to sex.

"Well, you have to."

Not his best. He might as well just do whatever she wanted right now—or whatever she thought she wanted. She needed to eat something.

"Later."

Tearing his gaze away again, he focused on the ceiling and his ability to think improved. Slightly. "You have to put those things away. They're hypnotic."

Things? He could practically feel his IQ dropping.

"So if I sway from side to side, like a metronome, will you become suggestible so I can take advantage of you? I've tried everything else."

Dante couldn't not laugh at her question, but he

closed his eyes to keep from looking—not that he couldn't picture it just fine on his own.

Then he felt the edge of the mattress moving rhythmically against his leg.

"You're doing it, aren't you?"

"Maybe."

Taking advantage of his lack of vision and the confidence rolling through her, Lise crawled the short distance to where he stood and sat on her knees, close enough to press against him if she decided to.

"I can feel you," he whispered, opening his eyes to find her kneeling in her panties in front of him.

Good. She could always feel him nearby too.

No matter the clumsy seduction she'd made under less than ideal circumstances, she'd truly wanted him. Still did.

It should've probably sent her running for the hills how incapable she was of ignoring her attraction for the man now. How utterly tempted she was to accept his proposal, when the fact that she couldn't even decide if he was fully trustworthy should've had her on a plane to a different time zone.

And no part of that fear diminished how badly she wanted him.

"You can feel me," she whispered back. "I need you to feel me." The look in his eyes stopped her words, stopped her breath. His fingertips trailed down the side of her face, and then caught and tucked a lock of her hair behind her ear.

Not another word passed her lips.

With a groan, he reached for her, his hand shooting round the back of her neck and he tugged her up to meet him as he leaned in, mouth hot and hungry on hers.

Her arms shot under his and around his shoulders, and she rose on her knees so their bared torsos melded together. The same skin contact that had comforted and connected now buzzed, heated. She recalled the feel of the smattering of crisp, dark hair on his chest, rasping against her cheek as she'd wept. The trail of her tears that had cut rivers in it, sticking the hair to his skin. The way he'd held her as if he couldn't get her close enough.

In those moments, she'd only really been able to feel and comprehend the need to be close, to be held, and had translated that as a need for sex.

But that was very different from the excitement that surged through her now.

She still felt connected, above and beyond the physical sensation of his body against hers. A connection she didn't really want all that much, but which had the power to put her fears and doubts out of her mind. At least for a time.

His hands slid down her back, strong, deft fingers exploring every contour, every curve, while his masterful mouth led her in a dance she couldn't help but fall into.

When he reached the band of her panties, his hands dove in, cupping, squeezing, and lifting her those last inches that kept their lower bodies from aligning.

One moment she was pressed to him, breathless, clutching at the smooth, muscled strength of his shoulders, and the next, the world tilted and he fell with her.

The mattress absorbed their impact, and Dante broke from her mouth to wind a scorching trail of kisses down her neck to the breasts she'd finally used purposefully to tempt with rather than hide.

Both hands cupped and pressed the mounded flesh together, squeezing, exploring their weight and the way they moved, the way they firmed and responded to even the lightest flick of his tongue across her nipples.

When he finally captured one and drew it into his mouth, she arched off the bed, her moans becoming a plea for more, for everything.

# CHAPTER EIGHT

DANTE CAUGHT THE taunting pink panties and nearly tore them in his need to get them off. His own shorts came off in the next heartbeat and he took a few deep breaths, trying to force himself to slow down.

Wasn't working.

He'd lain awake holding her most of the day, and couldn't banish the sight of her standing there, crying and shaking, on his veranda.

The leg at his hip swiveled and wrapped around him, a squeeze urging him on by making his hardness glide through the wet heat waiting for him.

It was all he could take. Locking with her gaze, he gripped himself and rushed into her, his hips not stopping until they met the backs of her bent thighs.

Once at the hilt, he closed his eyes and a hard shudder ran through him. He didn't deserve her sweet body. It felt like forgiveness and she couldn't forgive him for something that he couldn't bear to confess to her. It would be the fastest way to get her out of his life entirely. And he wanted her in it. It was better with her in it. And he'd make her life better too. He'd make all this up to her.

Lise had lost her virginity long before she'd decided she couldn't bear a romantic relationship, but it had been a long time. The intensity of such an intimate act while staring into his eyes deepened the connection, and although she understood that the shudder was a good sign, closing his eyes to her dampened the connection. And she needed it.

"Please." She whispered one word, and his eyes opened, though there was worry there. Guilt. "I like it when you see me."

Even as the words came out, she slid her hands down his back, urging him to move since he'd planted her beneath him.

A nod communicated his understanding, and he leaned closer still, close enough that she could see nothing but him, breathe nothing but him, and he started to move.

As if his body refused to bend to his will, his hips gave spontaneous jerks that disrupted his rhythm, always timed with a gasp and stuttering breath. The sense of connection she'd been unable to ignore between them seemed to surge. It wasn't just sex. It wasn't just purging hours of desperation from her heart. It wasn't just fear of wanting to be with him—because she did. She wanted to be with him.

And, oh, it might make her feel better if she could get some kind of guarantee that he wouldn't change, that he wasn't being someone other than who he truly was. She could say yes…if she believed in her ability to judge as much as she believed in how much she loved to just be around him.

His ragged breaths and groans sounded like music to her, and when he looked into her eyes she could believe him. She wanted to believe him. She even felt a surge of something warm and healing.

But she couldn't make herself focus on it, decide if it was true or real. Pressure had built in her to such an ache that she had no room in her mind to spare for thinking, for trying to understand what she saw in his eyes. There was only sensation so keen she nearly asked him to stop.

But then he kissed her again, devouring with his mouth in time with the starved pace he set with his hips. Everything went bright, like a lightning strike, and that ache exploded, curling her toes against his muscled butt, contracting every muscle in her body as she clung to him and rode wave after wave of pleasure.

He fell with her, and by the time he'd spent within her, she could tell his strength was leaving him. With shaking arms, and likely the last of his strength, he rolled with her to his back, keeping her anchored to him, buried inside her, urging her to rest her cheek back against his shoulder in sleep.

Having slept the day away, Lise didn't want to listen to her body, which felt drugged and weak. Sleep would not happen, not yet.

Though his arms were still tight around her, she leaned up enough to look down at him, and feeling her change in position Dante opened his eyes. His member, softening now, stayed inside her, and that connection persisted.

"Do you still want me?"

"Yes. But I'm going to need a few minutes to recover."

She might be high on pleasure, she might be trusting too much, but it couldn't hurt to ask. "I mean as a wife."

He nodded slowly, like he just wasn't sure where

her question was leading, or what she wanted him to say. "You're perfect for me."

"I want to meet your family. It's important that I meet them, see how they are. They're a big draw for me. I need to know they're the right kind of people, that they'll love and cherish our children if something happens to us. I need to know them before I make any decisions."

He nodded again, the worry leaving his face. "I'll set it up. We'll do it this week. Wednesday."

By the time Wednesday rolled around, Dante was so tense he could've abandoned the whole plan—marriage, children, introducing Lise to his brothers…

"It's good that you don't have super-strength," Lise said randomly, sitting in the passenger seat of his car as he drove her to the weekly inventory at his family's bodega.

"Why's that?"

"Because you'd have broken the steering wheel by now, and we'd probably be on fire, inside burning, twisted wreckage."

He looked at his hands, neatly placed at the nine and three positions—as updated safety guidelines suggested in a post-airbags world.

The white knuckles weren't part of the guidelines.

"I'm not going to mention the club or what we're possibly plotting to do together. Even if they put the thumbscrews on me, all they'll get is that we met at work, and that you asked me out after accidentally discovering one day that I had a waistline, and that you make a mean margarita."

"That's not what happened."

"Yes, it is."

"No, it's not, and you can't say that because they'll wonder how I learned you have a waistline. Which isn't even what happened."

"What happened, then?"

"You stopped hiding in your massively oversized scrubs and let people see you for once."

"So you didn't notice me before because of workplace camouflage. Got it."

"You know you did it. And picking a fight right now is not the way to prepare for meeting anyone. Stick to the plan. Don't sass it up with comments about your waistline or self-deprecating anything."

"Just cut off all my conversation starters."

"I did."

"Why do you assume I'm going to fail? Do you

find me unlikeable while also finding me minxy? Or are you truly just lusting after my irresistibly vacant womb?"

"I don't expect you to fail. I like you. And you're still picking a fight."

"You're making me crazy!" She rumbled out a breath between pursed lips and leaned back in her seat.

"I love my brothers, but when we're all together we can become…a handful." Dante gave an answer that, while not the entire truth, was still true in part. As Lise was the first woman he'd ever brought to meet them, they were going to be more jovial and energetic than usual.

"You're afraid I'll think they're not fit to raise my future children?"

"It's possible."

"But you don't think that."

"I have no doubt that any of them would take our children in and be wonderful parents. Alejandro is already a father, Santiago and Rafael are about to become fathers. But you might need to meet them more than once to be convinced. And I'm ready to get started. I know you are too. A person who isn't hot to be a mother would never have a sorted spreadsheet of sperm donors."

"Actually, it's not a spreadsheet anymore. I sorted it all down to one donor. And then I made a pros and cons list for both of you."

"As a backup plan?"

"No. As the first plan. You came along second. But I'm just continuing the planning part for Plan A. Relax, me figuring out who could be the one doesn't mean he will be."

Dante pulled into a gravel parking lot beside a quaint little market, and the presence of his brother's cars confirmed they were the last to arrive.

"Try not to mention sperm donors either."

She groaned. "I'm not going to. You brought it up!"

"And however my pros and cons list worked out, pretend you really like me."

"I do like you, doofus." She grabbed him by the cheeks and leaned up to kiss him full on the mouth. Not the sort of kissing he'd really like from her, but a playful, warm, and entertainingly bratty smooch that left him with a smile despite the knot in his gut.

Then they climbed out and the unease returned. He reached for her hand and sought to feign his usual collected self.

That she'd come to meet him after her time with

baby Eli and then conjured up this request to meet his family assured him she'd still say yes. Even if she'd picked her favorite sperm donor. But usually he felt more confident about these sorts of things.

"Rafe—Rafael. Santi—Santiago. Alejandro," she murmured under her breath just as he opened the door.

He paused to add, "They're all at Buena Vista or Seaside hospitals."

Dante listed spouse names, lest she think he'd forgotten they existed entirely. Pulling open the back entrance, he ushered her out of the still bright sunshine into a dimly lit, windowless room.

Oh, this could go terribly. And the way Dante was stressing out over it made her very first expression a lie. She smiled—a forced smile, a lying smile—and hoped it passed as cheerful.

Certainly with something as nerve-racking as it was to meet the family of someone you were dating, they'd understand her forced cheer if anyone caught on.

This had all been her idea, and she shouldn't be the one being judged as pass or fail—she was here with a mission: find out if the Valentinos would be suitable guardians or not. But knowing how close they all were meant they'd be doing the same to make sure she was good enough for their last bachelor brother.

Probably.

She'd had so little experience of dealing with positive family dynamics, her supposition was entirely based on some basic psychology classes she'd taken while working on her degree, and re-runs of old sitcoms.

"Hey!" A chorus of greetings rang out from around the room, and though she answered back, she stopped moving immediately and had to be propelled inside by the man behind her.

"Hey, dozer, I'm sunblind here. Don't plow me over some innocent bystander before my eyes adjust to the darkness." Great start! Probably exactly an example of the kind of conversation she should not be aiming for. Should've added a "sweetheart" or something.

The sound of laughter came from all corners—except one. Dante did let go of her hand, but only so he could wrap his arm around her waist and pull her back against him. "Wouldn't dream of disrupting inventory so selfishly, *corazón*."

Of course *he* thought to add a "sweetheart" to his statement. Must do better.

The sound of jostling cans preceded a line of remarkably tall and attractive dark-haired men appearing before her.

"Good lord, you all look like that."

Yet more words she should've thought through first but which instead flew out reflexively as her eyes adjusted enough to make out one stupidly handsome man after another.

Dante was going to lose his mind and call things off before they even got to the introductions.

"Like what?" he asked smoothly from behind her, but there was a tiny warning in his tone.

"Er…like…" She tilted her head and swiveled to look at the handsome devil looming over her shoulder. "Let's go with handsome? Yeah. Handsome."

Dante didn't buy it, she could tell from the flex of his jaw, but she heard female laughter off in the recesses of the dim room and knew at least someone got it.

He introduced his brothers—lined up eldest to youngest as if they'd been drilling and practicing all day—then asked if everyone was there. Alejandro she recognized from the hospital, but she had never worked with him, or even known his name. He'd always been just some mysterious attractive man in scrubs.

Three women appeared—a dark-haired beauty with a baby and two blondes with babies on board. Kiri, she found, was another face from her hospital—someone else she'd never met.

"Nice to meet you all." Lise waved to each as names were matched to faces.

"Here, Lise." Kiri offered up the baby in her arms. "Hold the littlest Valentino and come have a sit with us while the men count."

Lise hesitated for a moment—was every person in the room a doctor but her? At least Dante had to let her know the baby had had a heart transplant in recent months, but that was a different kind of trauma than baby Eli had undergone. This little angel was peaceful.

Dante let go of her waist and she stepped forward to take the baby. "I'm sure Dante told me his name, but I'm blanking. That's what happens when I say a bunch of really stupid things in quick succession."

"Gervaso." Kiri laughed, and they all wandered toward a clump of folding chairs and sturdy-looking boxes.

Lise left the folding chairs to the belly brigade

and perched on a stack of twelve-packs of some variety of beverage.

"We were just hearing that Dante has never brought a woman round. But I'm fairly certain that's another trait the whole family shares," one of them said.

Cassie!

Lise felt proud for remembering anything at this point. "Maybe it's genetic."

The baby in her arms gurgled, and Lise found herself momentarily transfixed.

She and Dante hadn't been careful when they'd been together. Could've made the decision for them. Or maybe just complicated things. If she found out she was pregnant and still wasn't sure, would she feel compelled to marry him? She didn't consider herself a traditional kind of person, but mostly that was because she'd never been able to picture herself capable of marriage.

Gervaso fisted his eyes sleepily and she cuddled him a little closer.

If it became complicated, there was no one to blame but herself, as she'd begged for him. Even after he'd said, no, thank you.

"Lise?" one of the women said her name and

she pulled out of her own thoughts to focus on the talking people.

"I'm sorry. He's just so sweet. It's hard to look away."

Kiri took it as a compliment, and nodded. "I was asking if you ever worked other surgical teams or if you'd had specialty training for Neuro?"

Oh, work stuff. She had to reseat her intention to form complete sentences, then let herself be drawn into the conversation as much as she could.

They all seemed so energized by being together, while she must look like a timid recluse.

The only ones not speaking much were her and Dante. He counted cans, marked info on a ledger attached to a clipboard, and watched everything and everyone else—but most especially her. And it wasn't the dark, sexy kind of watching that made her tingle in interesting places. It was the kind of watching that made her nervous, made her say stupid things.

The women tried to draw her into their conversations here and there, but usually all she managed were the sort of answers that did nothing to keep the conversation going. This was a meeting where she wanted to measure them up—and also to see how they interacted with Dante, thinking maybe it could put her at ease about the decision she'd already made and now spent time trying to talk herself out of.

"How long have you all known one another?" she asked them, trying to get her bearings, trying to figure out how long it had taken them to bond to the point that they practically chirped with enthusiasm and amusement at one another while talking.

They gave a series of months that shocked her. Not at all long, and already so attached and friendly. It was like watching sisters…

"It's a lot to meet the whole family at once." Saoirse extended an olive branch, which was jumped on by each woman in turn, all agreeing.

"I did this a few weeks ago. Trust me, I remember the tension all too well, and there were only four for me to meet. You have two more since there are six of us now. Plus Dante, but you already know him." Cassie had reached out to her again. Kind women. All of them.

"Dante," a male voice called, getting Lise's attention—getting everyone's attention.

"You look like you're about to lower the boom on someone." Rafe. The twin! Lise identified him, felt fleeting pride, moved past it…

She would never have looked at them and thought of them as twins. Aside from them all being handsome men with similar coloring, they each had a look all their own. But somehow, in all that, the most handsome one of all was the one she might have landed if she decided to land and he was still amenable to the landing...after all this.

"He's afraid we're going to embarrass him in front of *la rubia bonita*," teased Alejandro.

The pretty blonde. That could be any one of three. Or two, really.

"Alejandro!" Saoirse yelled at him, and it took Lise a second to realize she wasn't his wife.

Ugh, she might never get this.

They all thought Dante was tense, expecting *them* saying the wrong thing? Poor people, worried for nothing. He was worried about her messing everything up. And she hadn't really done anything to calm that fear so far, what with one stupid thing after another shooting like popcorn from her reckless mouth.

The ribbing seemed to relax him. Dante shrugged, "I'm trying to convince her I'm the last decent unmarried man left in Miami."

"She works with you—she knows better."

So they weren't asking *How did you meet?* questions because they already knew. Had he prepped them too? Were there any forbidden topics from their end?

"And now she knows you're the ugly one. Should've married her before you brought her around your handsome brothers."

He bent, snatched something small and shiny from the floor, and chucked it at Alejandro. "Laugh it up, *flaca loco*. You're all taken. She'll just have to settle for the ugly one."

The good-natured banter and laughing did more for her than all the attempts to include her or put her at ease.

Something else was said—in Spanish, so she didn't get it—but it resulted in a roar of laughter from around the room.

In her arms, Gervaso startled and then began to cry. For the briefest second, panic rose in her, but before she could even think about asking what other ways were safe to hold him, Alejandro put his clipboard down and headed toward them.

"Is he getting fussy?" he asked while showing her his hands, indicating his desire to hold and comfort his son, and she wasn't about to argue.

Lifting the red-faced, squirming bundle, she

eased him into his father's arms and laughed a little. "I swear I didn't pinch him."

Her silly explanation earned her an odd look, then the man smiled and lifted the frightened baby to his shoulder to walk and bounce—something she'd tried and failed to comfort Eli with, but which worked for Alejandro.

On his next pass, when he could keep his voice lower, Alejandro explained. "He's basically healed now, but if something causes him to move sharply or suddenly, I think his chest aches. A change in position helps."

"I'm sure that having his daddy hold him helps too," she said, but then rose and slipped around him, heading for the flat of cans the new daddy had abandoned. A quick scan to make sure she understood the system, and she followed to where he'd left off and resumed inventory.

"Hey, she counts!" Santiago wasn't quiet, but he did keep himself a few decibels further down from frightening-the-baby level, and pointed at the other women, turning his teasing onto them. "I hope you three see what a good example looks like." And finished with, "Lise, you're hired. Marry him tomorrow."

The teasing words caused her to blush, but she

laughed too—half in appreciation of the inclusive ribbing, half in nervousness.

The ribbing, the counting, the welcoming feeling they all gave—whatever Dante had felt compelled to do to provide for them must've weighed on him if it had turned him into the sourpuss of this lot.

It wasn't fair that he'd carried all that on his own. And now that she'd met his family, she couldn't even picture a scenario where they wouldn't share the load.

Could people change? If he had her helping him lead a transparent life, could he let go of all that? Or was it buried too deep to be dug out now?

She was probably grasping at straws to comfort herself. This was probably how people made themselves blind to the flaws of their loved ones and partners.

The only thing she knew with absolute certainty was that people who adopted and fell in love with a seriously ill baby were good people. She could trust her still hypothetical children to these people. And they didn't walk on eggshells around him—he'd even responded in the same manner.

The visit lasted about two hours, and by the end not only had Gervaso been passed around to get gentle affection from everyone in attendance—including Dante—but the rest had passed her cell phone around, taking selfies for identification purposes and putting their data into her contacts. Six new people in her Miami acquaintances.

Dante waited until Lise had closed her car door then turned toward her, searching her profile in the glow of the streetlights.

Why wasn't she looking at him?

From his disadvantaged position, he could make out pinched brows and a set jaw.

Worried, or thoughtful?

"Did they pass?" he asked finally, reaching over to gently turn her face toward him. "You got everyone's number."

"They're lovely people," she said, reaching up to take the hand on her chin. She squeezed it then, gently but firmly, lowered it to the console separating them.

Despite her complimentary words, she didn't look excited or even resolved.

"But...?"

"But nothing. They're really great. It was a little overwhelming at first, I was nervous and everything I said sounded like some kind of ridiculous, hammy line from a badly written B-movie." Then she drew in a deep breath, exhaled slowly, and added, "I don't think I've ever been in one room with that many people who were all related. At least, not for any length of time. It's a lot."

If she were retreating again, he'd have to make it harder to do. Despite the fact that she'd disengaged his hand from her face, he caught one of her small hands and held it. True to the agreement of one night, no promises, she'd distanced herself after leaving his home last Saturday. But he'd expected this meeting to turn that distance around—or at least he'd hoped it would. He'd hoped it would lead to an easy yes, and even now, looking back, he couldn't see any reason that the word wasn't already rushing from her lips.

He concentrated on the connection with her hand, and listening. And squeezing to show support. "So?"

"No."

"You're saying no?" he asked as she firmly reclaimed her hand.

"No. I'm not saying no to that. I'm saying I still need some time to sort all this out. I need to be smart about this decision. I can't just fall in love with a sweet little baby in my arms and the truly humbling amount of love circulating in that room. I have to be as rational and smart as I can be in this."

"More pros and cons lists?" he asked, trying not to be irritated at having to abide by another's schedule again. When he made decisions, he immediately began pursuing them. That's how he operated. He'd chosen Lise, and now he wanted to make some measurable headway, but it seemed like a perpetual holding pattern.

"Maybe. Though the past week has added a number of pros to your list. That's not the problem. It's not even the number of cons, it's just the type. Just the one, really."

As they both knew what she was referring to, Dante said nothing else, just started the car and backed out. Soon they were back on the road, and both seemed to have run out of words to say for the evening.

If she couldn't move past the way he handled The Inferno, he would have to cut his losses, no matter how fantastic the sex, no matter how much he liked her.

# CHAPTER NINE

DANTE WANTED AN ANSWER. After meeting them, she'd needed more time. So he'd waited. Waited and become very aware that he no longer had enough patience for a long con.

Waiting usually felt strong—it made people look at the things he'd told them differently. They had time for ideas to percolate, their opinions to change, their enthusiasm to build...until they finally came to him.

Then they'd had their usual three-day weekend in preparation for the unholy, long-hours of their four-day workweek. So he'd expected that by Monday, or Tuesday at the latest, she'd have come to him with her answer.

Another inventory day had come and gone in the meantime, and she'd avoided him like a leper in all ways outside work during that time, but he craved time with her. His body had already signed on the dotted line—his wife, the woman he was supposed to be naked with as much as possible. But it wasn't just physical, he missed her.

In the last fifteen minutes of the second Thursday since the bodega, Dante finally worked it out. He wasn't the one in power here. She was, and his patience officially ran out.

He summoned her.

Five days working together in that time, and standing shoulder to shoulder with her in surgery every morning. He'd seen her five days out of eight, and was available to her every day.

There was a knock at his private office door and Dante barked, "Come!"

Scowling, Lise stepped in and closed the door, her arms folded under her breasts in a way that, yes, made her look cross with him, but also distracted him with an extraordinary amount of cleavage.

"How can you possibly still be thinking about this?" he asked, one arm flying toward the ceiling in a rush of frustration. "You're smart enough to have sorted this out by now!"

"Is that *really* how you want to start this conversation?"

Dante ran both his hands over his face, blew out a sharp breath and forced himself around the desk to sit on the sofa. It was the first time he'd ever been angry with her, but she was right. This wasn't the time to lose his cool.

She watched him until he made himself relax, and only then did she cross the office to sit beside him. Her soft, warm thigh pressed against his, distracting him.

*Don't touch her yet. Hands under control.*

"I needed time apart from you for the idea to settle without all…this." She gestured to their thighs, touching and tingling even though separated by at least two layers of cloth. "Attraction clouds my thinking."

He opened his mouth to speak, but she cupped her hand over his mouth, the soft hollow of her palm shutting him up.

"And then I had my cycle too…sort of. And I really wanted to make sure I wasn't being emotional because of that either, since we went without protection. I needed space so I could trust that my decision wasn't influenced by a massive amount of desire to go to bed with you again, or fear of a protracted legal battle if I got pregnant and was too afraid to get married."

Dante urged her hand to his lap and kept hold

of it, but since she still had words rushing from her mouth, he held his tongue.

"I wasn't slighting you, I was just trying to trust my own decision. And you're kind of like a bull. If I had given you an opening you could in any way interpret to mean *please convince me*, you'd have resumed convincing me, and you're very convincing. I just needed me in my head to make the decision. So don't yell at me about this in the office!"

Her voice rose at the end and she scowled, then fell silent.

Before she'd even gotten to the end of her own wordy tirade Dante had felt the tension draining from the back of his neck. "All right. So we're agreed. Engaged."

A flash of guilt on her face, and she pulled her gaze away, a negative noise rumbling in her throat.

The tension returned as she pulled her hand away.

"Your family is wonderful. A huge comfort. But I do have just one little other condition."

"Lise…"

"I can see you're testy, and I know you're not used to being made to wait for anything, so I'm going to overlook it right now and not kick you in the junk because you're not the only one who's stressing out over this. My condition is for your benefit too."

"What is it?"

He wouldn't yell. He wouldn't yell. He wouldn't yell.

"I want to be pregnant before we announce anything about us. I've seen enough to know that fertility issues can affect marriage, and women who are otherwise perfectly healthy can find it impossible to conceive. The truth is, we don't know that I can conceive a child. If I couldn't hold up my end, it wouldn't be fair to you. This marriage will be unconventional already—there's no room for us not to get what we want. And I'd rather not have a divorce to deal with on top of my dream of children breaking—should it come to that. So it's for both our benefits."

Every now and then Lise could catch a glimpse of what Dante was thinking or feeling before he outright told her. Yelling and big emotional displays—like when she'd stepped into his office after he'd demanded her presence—were easy. She picked up on the anger before she'd got into the room. But now that the moment had passed he'd reverted to the cool, implacable man who frustrated her.

She couldn't tell if he approved of her condition or was about to unleash an objection on her. Maybe if she said something else, he'd speak. "When I get pregnant, I will accept your ring."

"No. Engagement now," he said. "If you want to avoid a divorce if you can't get pregnant, then we'll marry after you're pregnant, but I want this settled."

"Why?"

"Because it fits your needs and mine. I'm tired of waiting. I've been patient."

"This was you being patient?"

"Believe it or not. We'll move you in on Saturday."

"What about my cottage? I don't want it to sit empty. There are vandals and arsonists... All that and loss of homeowner's insurance if it's unoccupied for a whole month."

"Fine. We'll spend some nights there and work on getting it sold."

Dante reached for her closest hand and she turned her palm toward his so she could link fingers with him. It was a small gesture, but once the digits entwined he lifted his eyes to hers. "That also settles your arguments."

Lise nodded, but it was in her to make sure he understood the leap she was making. "I'm still not at ease with everything."

"The best way to get used to the idea is to jump into it."

"I guess." She was adaptable, but the fear still lingered that this would all go wrong. "I don't want there to be any guns in the house. Not even locked up in a safe, not there at all. Taser if you feel the need to be armed."

Maybe she needed to prove something to herself.

"I can live with that," Dante said easily enough. "I can compromise, see? And with three of our four parents dying from gunshot wounds, I have no problem with that."

He stood and gestured for her to stand up, and it was all too easy to step in and lean against him. She'd missed him, and working at his side all week had been one temptation after another. If the week to think was anything to go by, this was the only sensible decision to make. In one swoop she got a father for her children, an extended family to love and protect them, a lover, and an occasional friend when he wasn't infuriating her.

Rising up abruptly, she pressed her mouth to his. Dante needed no persuading. His arms tightened around her and mashed her to him as he took control and deepened the kiss, turning it into a promise for the weeks to come.

The day was over, they could stay, get naked on the second version of that same uncomfortable leather sofa she'd seen in his possession.

Despite her attempts to get distance enough to make good decisions, echoes of the pleasure from their one night had rolled around in her thoughts all week, haunting her, teasing her, probably corrupting her judgment despite her best efforts.

She just couldn't keep going like she had been for the past three years. She had to take a chance on people, and even if it all went badly with Dante, their children would be tied to his family. The wives would probably still be her friends.

It felt like counting on failure to think that way, but it helped her actually be able to even try to say yes. Trust came hard, but she wanted to trust him. After all those ideas that having a baby could alleviate her loneliness, having spent time with babies the past few weeks had changed her mind.

She still wanted a baby, but she needed to have someone to talk to as well. Now. Not in eighteen years when they could hold a satisfying adult conversation.

Hanging out with other men might not even alleviate it—she'd never felt that spark of life with anyone else. It was sink or swim time. Even if she'd be lying to herself if she tried to pretend she could tie her life to another's and ever really let her guard down fully.

A knock sounded at the door and Lise leapt back from him with the power of a guilty sneak, and landed almost outside his reach.

"Dr. Valentino?"

Office manager's voice came through the door. Lise identified it and jabbed a finger toward his desk. They wouldn't be making out if he were behind his desk.

She moved to the door and smiled at the nice lady, Kathy, she found on the other side. Kathy reported last-minute messages of the day, a consultation request from Seaside for tomorrow, and that the office was otherwise locked up. The woman, whom Lise had liked very much since her transfer, gave her a suspicious eye but then politely wished them both a good weekend and left.

"She knows," Lise muttered as soon as the door closed. "Or the hospital gossip reached her."

"She's been with me since I came to Buena Vista. She's not going to say anything. Besides, we're engaged. She'll find out soon enough. Your engagement ring will give it away."

In an attempt to leave her cottage in still livable condition, Lise only moved things she absolutely needed to live for a week into Dante's house—scrubs, some casual clothing, and sleepwear.

She could have claimed it was because she wanted to make sure they spent some nights there—and that was partly true—but there was another, less cooperative or optimistic reason.

Now that she'd decided to give a relationship with Dante a try, she needed a safety net. She hadn't had a serious relationship ever, not really. She'd dated, at least prior to moving to Miami, but those had been very superficial relationships. The only time she'd ever lived with someone, they'd shared genes.

With the last of her clothes now stashed in the bureau in the spare room, she had nothing to keep busy. The transition was going to be weird, and she accepted that it would take some time to get used to, but she'd thought that Dante would've been happy to see her when she arrived. He'd taken her keys, moved her car into the garage and carried in a few odds and ends she couldn't make in one trip, but past that he'd returned to the medical journal he'd been reading and let her get on with things.

No hug. No kiss. He hadn't even smiled at her, and he should be happy—he'd convinced her to do exactly what he wanted.

With that kind of reception, she felt compelled to try and tidy the spare bedroom, just in case.

The house had four bedrooms—the master bedroom where Dante slept and three other rooms, two of them still entirely empty and this one with a bedroom suite and a big exercise machine that cluttered up the floor space. The machine could've easily gone into one of the empty rooms, but it was here, beside the bed.

Dante had ordered another bureau made to match the one in his room...*their* room?...so she'd only be coming in here for clothes until that one arrived. The idea seemed weirder to her than her clothes living in a room away from her. Having a bureau to match his felt like pressure.

Lise gave herself a mental shake and went back

to the living area. Off the main room, she saw Dante sitting at the kitchen table, and the smell of some kind of meaty goodness beckoned her into that room.

Still reading the journal.

She joined him at the table. This was happening, and if part of her decision to give it a try had hinged on the fact that she was lonelier now without him, Lise wanted his company. Now that she had keys, the whole situation felt like a block tower built by five-year-olds—shaky, unstable, and a little scary, even if she could hardly even admit that to herself.

"I found the instructions for the security system so you can have your own PIN entered."

Talking!

"Where?" Lise asked, ready to fly off and get the idiot sheet, wherever it might be hiding.

Dante gestured behind her to the center island, and kept reading that blasted journal.

If she got up and retrieved the instructions, the conversation would shut down entirely, and she needed it. Maybe he needed it too. The man was behaving so oddly she had to think this was just as weird for him as it was for her.

He'd always at least smiled at her. Had that only been for show? His way to prove compatibility?

Skip it. He wasn't telling her lies if he wasn't talking, and he was home. It was weird at the start of anything new.

"Did you get settled okay?" he asked, finally looking up from whatever he was reading. In that moment she was so pathetically thankful she could've cried.

"I didn't bring that much. We'll need to go to the cottage soon, but I'm stashed away for now."

"Good. We'll go in a few days. I was wondering if you'd want to replicate your nursery design in one of the other rooms, or if you wanted to hire a decorator to take care of it?"

Still talking. He'd looked back to the journal, but he was multitasking and only looking at her sporadically.

"I could do it. Paint it…though, actually, a happy little mural with ducks in a pond maybe, on one of the big walls…that might be nice. Otherwise, when the cottage sells, and after I'm pregnant, I'll just want to move the furniture from there over here."

"However you want to handle it," Dante said, and she knew he offered as a way to help her feel at home there, even if it would've been nice to have him include himself in the decision, or even in the actual project. "The pulled pork in the oven will be done reheating in a few minutes, along with the sweet potato wedges."

"You cooked?"

"I just reheat usually. Carmelita makes me food enough to last the week. Kind of like home-made frozen dinners. I pick them up on inventory nights. Good food. Easy for me to handle with a busy schedule. And she convinced me I needed to let her do it for me after Cassie and Rafe got married. Think she decided the project was doable since it wouldn't need to be repeated for the other three of us. I relented when she agreed to let me pay her for it."

"Wow, wish I'd met her."

"You will."

"We never talked about how we were going to merge lives."

Dante put the journal down then and met her eyes over the table, "What do you mean?"

"Well, like the food. Will you want me to cook and do those traditional wife types of things?" She didn't mention his failure to seem at all ex-cited she'd made the move to his house. Sort of, at least. He'd just stuck with the easier topics, like the one he'd brought up with the nursery.

"If you want to." He shrugged. "Doesn't matter to me. I imagine we could keep doing it like this later. The food's good, and I'm sure the extra money helps her out. Maybe split up—"

"I'm not a good cook. I have one thing I do really well: lemon pepper chicken salad. That's one thing that's cooked—one very simple thing—and lots of chopping. You probably cook better than I do."

"Settled, then. If Carmelita's up for it. If she's not, I'm sure we can find someone else to provide the same kind of arrangement." He stood, grabbed a towel and used it to move the aluminum trays from the oven to the stove top. "What else?"

"What's your club schedule like?" she asked next, to at least keep him talking to her.

"I go in two nights per week usually. Thursday to play, Monday to meet with the manager and go over things for the week. There's an occasional weekend visit, but it's only as needed. The manager is good at what he does."

With the food out of the oven, Lise went to the cabinets to find plates, glasses, and cutlery, then brought the plates to the stove.

Once they sat down, Lise watched him return to his journal and his silence, and tried not to worry about it.

In the silence, those other questions she wanted to avoid on their first night officially together gained ground. And she couldn't give voice to any of them.

If she started asking any of the thousand questions she had about him, they wouldn't be done before it was time for bed. He radiated unease already, even if he sounded confident about everything. Baring the depth of her doubts would only start a fight on her first night in her new home.

*Save the prying for things that mattered*—mostly things he'd be doing outside the home. She didn't need to be more vigilant than that, she hoped.

"You've been quiet tonight," she said finally, but still couldn't bring herself to admit how badly she needed a hug from him or some kind of reassurance. "Are you well?"

Cowardly way to beat around the bush, but limiting what she'd allow herself to ask had a way of limiting her. This was only a gentle foray into more personal subjects.

"Just doing my homework."

He made it sound so impersonal, even if he could've found a better night for homework. Yes, he needed to be up to date on the most recent medical studies, but tonight?

It took everything in her not to sigh, frustrated with both of them. She'd been living alone for years and she couldn't amuse herself while he read for work?

Ridiculous.

After she finished eating, Lise volunteered to clean up. He'd been an island unto himself for twenty minutes, but he heard her and cleared out of the kitchen. She could at least acquaint herself with the space. If they weren't going to do much bonding tonight, she'd bond with the kitchen.

The first strains of Dante's piano reached her over the sound of running water, and she quickly wrenched the tap off so she could hear whatever he was playing at that baby grand in the living room.

It was music she didn't know, but immediately liked. There was a simplicity to the score that left her thinking of a music box from a fairy-tale straight out of Grimm—tinkling with the potential for lightness, but instead buoyed by something darker.

If he wasn't going to talk to her, Lise wouldn't deprive herself of hearing him play. She followed the music and walked in as quietly as she could to keep from interrupting.

The cock of his head at her quiet approach confirmed that he knew she was there, but he kept playing and she stayed at the sofa until the last ringing notes faded in the air.

He turned on the stool and finally really looked at her, and there was that sadness again. But at least now when he focused on her he looked like he was actually seeing her.

She chanced speaking. "That was beautiful. So different from how you play at the club. What was it?"

"An arrangement of a song my mother used to sing."

"Your arrangement?"

He thought a second and then shrugged. "I guess."

"Is it a song from Heliconia?"

"Yes."

"Are you having second thoughts?" She just slipped that question in there among all the questions about the song.

He stood and looked at her for a long moment,

but stayed beside the piano, "About our arrangement?"

She nodded, then repeated her earlier statement. "You've been quiet tonight."

"No second thoughts. I sat to play, and that's what came out. The lullaby. Her favorite."

Lullaby?

"But that sounded so sad..."

With one hand, he closed the key cover on the piano, answering in a quiet voice, "That part was me."

Knowing how Dante felt about his family, she didn't need to ask for more clarification. They were embarking on an endeavor to start their own family—tonight was their first real night as a couple starting to work on the family they planned to build, and his mother would never be there to sing lullabies to any children their marriage created.

Her mother wouldn't either, but the difference was that Lise barely thought of her mother anymore. The thought that she'd never know her own grandchildren brought only the barest ache to Lise's chest, and was wholly something she could live with. But Dante still mourned his mom. The tears that burned her throat then were for him, for his whole family.

Their tragedy had pulled them so tightly to-gether that nearly half his life later it could still hurt him.

She swallowed, and walked directly to him, lift-ing her arms to catch around his shoulders. The intention had been to simply hug him, to offer comfort to him as he'd done to her after her long night with Eli—and she'd needed it. Her needs couldn't be met without her speaking up or act-ing. Acting was easier than putting her feelings on display through words that might show too much.

Dante immediately lowered his head and claimed her lips while his own arms crept around her waist and squeezed her to him.

He'd managed again not to answer her question about his quietness, and she began to wonder if he even realized he'd been different tonight. Did he only glimpse his own feelings when he began to play?

When he molded her to him and she could feel his body already responding, she gave up try-ing to sort him out and let him spin her from the piano to walk her backwards to the master suite.

Only seven in the evening, and already to bed. He wasn't ignoring her now.

His kisses, his hands, his body, the need she felt

coiling within him—all still there, comfortingly constant, but he still was different somehow.

Clothing went away, a soft bed welcomed them, and as quickly as he felt her ready, he plunged into her.

She saw it again, a shadow in his eyes as they joined together—worry and guilt—all mixed in with the pleasure neither of them could deny.

But he *was* different. And it felt like something she couldn't ignore, no matter how she knew things should be between them to be smart, to be safe—but she couldn't leave him in pain when she saw it bare and raw in his eyes.

Clasping his cheeks, she broke from his torturous kiss to whisper against his lips. "Please tell me what's wrong."

The only answer she got was a shake of his head, and a kiss deep enough to drug her senses.

Her body took the thick length of him over and over—hard, hot, and need-filled, until pleasure once more blocked out reason.

After a climax she felt all the way to the arches of her feet, he rolled away and reached immediately to put out the lights. But even with the electric incandescence gone, the last shards of daylight in the room enabled her to see him, to look again.

Her heart wanted to see him better. Her mind wanted it. Ignoring her body's desire to remain limp, she forced herself up onto her elbows and leveraged herself against him so she could look into his eyes.

"What are you doing?" he asked, watching her hands brace on his chest to steady her, his heart still galloping beneath her palms and her own burning in her breast.

And there was nothing there to see. No worry. No guilt. Not even a trace of the sadness that had hung on him before and after he'd played.

"Making sure you're okay," she whispered, starting to feel decidedly cranky again.

"I'm tired, but fine." He leaned in, kissed her gently, and then scooted down in the bed. "Early surgery in the morning. What time do you want to get up?"

Lise answered his question, said goodnight, and then rolled onto her side and away from him. If he said it was nothing, she'd just take him at his word until she had to face it again. He could live in denial, or he could live lying to her.

It couldn't be anything too bad this early so, whatever it was, he could deal with it alone for now.

He was a big boy, and could take care of himself.

But heaven help her if this wasn't just a case of growing pains.

# CHAPTER TEN

NOT SINCE RESIDENCY had Dante felt so tired—but this was for wholly pleasurable reasons.

Things had started out a little weird—having Lise around his house all the time, even though it was by his demand, was distracting.

Having her there in his bed every night couldn't have been better, no matter how tired it left him. Not only was it forward motion, but it was starting to feel more natural. He'd come home from the club Monday and she'd been there, at night when they drove home from work—separately as Lise insisted on waiting to share their engagement news until the ring was on her finger—having her there made him eager to get home.

He lifted himself off her and she opened her pale blue eyes. It always thrilled him to see her like that—a kind of sexual vacancy that robbed her of her senses. She made a noise of protest and he grabbed her naked hips and pulled, sliding her soft body to a slightly better position beneath him, so that when he hooked a hand under one of her knees and lifted she opened to him and he had space to settle between her luscious thighs.

That got him a smile.

It was going on a week since she'd moved in, and they were back in the beach house after two nights in her bed, in comfort so deep it'd felt like a vacation from his life.

Relaxing, comforting…almost enough to negate what hadn't happened that week—not announcing their engagement.

No ring, no announcement. People would expect something to exclaim over when they found out, she'd argued. And they'd look at them a little cockeyed if she'd worked for him for a week and suddenly become his fiancée.

He'd made it a point to buy a ring for her during the week, and now it was being sized. Next week it would be out to the world, official, and not something to back out of on a whim. Because that was how it felt right now. She was with him in the heat of every sexy moment, but she still didn't trust him and he felt the need to run everything he might say to her through his mind three times before letting the words out. The idea that she could lose her nerve was hard to ignore.

He settled back onto her, shifting his hips to make sure she felt him, and angled his head and caught her lower lip between his.

Then she yawned, and he let go, leaning up to look at her. "All right?"

"Mmm-hmm." She nodded, then reached her arms around his shoulders to pull him back against her.

He wanted her mouth, though having just seen her yawn, he barely got back into their marathon-like kissing groove when his own mouth rebelled, stretching out in a wide yawn.

"Bored or tired?"

"Tired," he answered immediately, and let his head loll forward against her shoulder.

"You know, we don't have to have sex tonight. I always want to, but we need to sleep too, and we have made it through my fertile time already, all without spraining anything or developing some kind of repetitive stress injury."

"You want to sleep?"

"I've napped in the exam rooms every day during lunch. I didn't think I was this dependent on a full eight hours, but I guess I am."

"Sleep deprivation," he mumbled against her neck, not caring to get any distance between them even if the night was starting to turn into a sex-less sleepover. "And being overworked doesn't help." Today had been a long day.

It only seemed allowable to him to let himself enjoy closeness and holding her if it involved other elements and could end in conception. They'd become engaged outside the usual expectations of marriage—their relationship worked fine with it based on sex and mutual interest, but the idea of affection outside sex didn't fit neatly into what he knew to be acceptable. Cuddling seemed to lean toward the wrong end of the spectrum. The messier end.

But they were so tired. Tonight didn't count.

The steady rise and fall of her chest made him smile against her neck. Already asleep. The woman could fall asleep faster than a narcoleptic.

The bedside lamp, still burning, let him lean back enough to see her face.

His kisses had turned her lips pink, and how she could drop off while still flushed with pre-climax arousal he couldn't even guess.

How had he failed to really notice for two years how pretty she was?

Mentally and physically, he was exhausted, but it was Thursday—there was no work tomorrow.

He could watch her a little longer, see if she talked in her sleep, then sleep in tomorrow. She couldn't grump at him about it if she didn't know.

Which was the same way he'd been appreciating her for the last two years, he realized. Only when no one was watching.

He'd seen her, but he'd shoved her into the box marked Work, and maintained his distance except for acceptable ways. Like requesting her for every surgery he could justify to himself.

He hadn't failed to see her because she'd always hidden in her oversized scrubs and ever-present scrub cap. He'd failed to allow any other context for her until she'd blithely wandered into his play yard. He'd limited her, and never acknowledged his attraction to her.

Maybe she was right about coming clean about the club to his brothers. Maybe he was limiting them in the same way.

Or maybe he was right to limit them. The Inferno's existence seemed like a gate he couldn't ever let them pass through without risking them finding out all the rest of the things he didn't want them to know. The dark things he had to hide.

His instincts had always protected them before.

He switched off the lamp and let himself lie half on her, his face buried in her long silky hair, and closed his eyes.

Dante jerked awake, his heart pounding, with no idea what had woken him.

He leaned off the soft beauty he'd been sleeping with, and noticed her eyes were open too, and she looked as confused as he felt. "Who's yelling?"

Yelling. That was what had woken him.

"What did they yell?" He sprang from the bed, grabbed his shorts and pulled them on.

"Your name."

"Man?" He crouched beside the bed, reached beneath and pulled out the baseball bat he only kept around for security—not that he'd ever needed it in this house, but old habits died hard.

"Man," she confirmed, stumbling around too, getting dressed.

"Where did the yell—?" He stopped when his name rang through the house again, answering the question before it got out."

"Stay here," he said, and, almost to the door, finally came awake enough to recognize the voice. He knew that voice. And there was something wrong with it.

*"Dios!"* He dropped the bat, wrenched open the bedroom door and broke into a dead run for the veranda.

Not one of his brothers, but at one point he might as well have been.

Middle of night, pitch-black out there, he couldn't see. He fumbled on the wall for the light and it glowed to life for him to see his old friend, flat on his back on the white-painted wooden deck.

Mateo was conscious, but wounded. He had a bloom of sticky dark red on the right side of his gray T-shirt.

"Lise!" He yelled for her, opening the door to help him. "I need you!"

Without a thought, he switched to Spanish as he crouched beside his friend. "Are you shot or was it a blade?"

*Please say blade.*

Wedging his arm under Mateo's head, he lifted him to a sitting position and held him so he could sling the man's arm around his own shoulders and get him off the ground.

"Gun," Mateo breathed when they stopped moving long enough for him to get enough air to speak.

They met Lise coming out, the bat he'd dropped held in her dainty hands, ready to defend him.

Seeing her there reminded him to switch back to English. "Get clean towels from the linen closet, alcohol, tweezers, the box of gloves in the bathroom, dental floss, a needle... Anything you think we can use. Then come to the kitchen."

"He's hurt." She took a few minutes to really wake up, but she'd been with it enough to grab her cell phone before rushing to his defense. She flipped it on to dial and Mateo swatted it out of her hand. It landed hard on the tile floor.

Dante grimaced. "Yes, and he needs our help. Get the supplies!"

Order given, he half carried Mateo into the kitchen, kicked the chairs away from the closest side of the table, and helped Mateo onto it and out of his shirt.

Lise returned with the towels and the supplies he'd thought to name to her, and after depositing them on the island she grabbed one of the towels and immediately went to apply pressure to the wound. She really didn't like this. Neither did he, but still he had to. At least she'd backed him up, but he couldn't even try to imagine what he'd say to explain this later.

"We need to call for an ambulance," she said. "You can't intend to remove a bullet in the kitchen."

"He needs my help. I owe him."

"It's a clean kitchen, but it's in no way sterile. Kitchens are bacteria havens. And you know as well as I do how much damage bullets can do once they go inside."

"Is that your wife, *jefe*?"

Lise blushed, clearly embarrassed. "Your English is just fine, isn't it? I'm sorry if I came across as inconsiderate to your pain. I didn't think you'd understand…for some reason."

"Because you just woke up," Dante finished for her, and jerked a few knives from the block until he found the paring knife.

"You're worried for your man. It's our wives who take care of the home. Your duty is to your family, *senora*," Mateo said. He was breathing a little better now that his only exertion was from pain. But he still could bleed out if they didn't get this right. "Don't be afraid. I didn't bring trouble to the *jefe*'s door. Just me."

"We're not married," Dante said, then to Lise, "If the bullet bounced around, he'd have bled out already. Boil water, then put this in it."

"Yet," Lise said, letting go of the towels and

paring knife he handed her, and he was so very glad to have been a stickler about his knives being a single piece of metal, no notches or joints for spores to lurk.

Yet? Oh, they were engaged. Later. He'd walk that back later.

"*Ayúdame, jefe*. I don't want to bleed to death."

"*Jefe* means boss, right?" Lise asked, as she dug a large glass bowl from the cupboard and began filling it from the tap.

"Not time for a Spanish lesson. Sterilize the knife," Dante ordered, and lifted the edge of the towel to peek at the wound. "I need more light." Replacing the towel, he moved one of Mateo's hands to apply his own pressure. "Press. I'll be right back."

In less than a minute he'd scrounged up a flashlight and some mild narcotics he'd had left over after injuring himself last year, and returned to find Lise taking Mateo's blood pressure. She'd found something else to help them.

"You're not allergic to anything, are you?"

"Just police."

Dante smiled a little at the old answer, shook a couple of the pills out, and grabbed a bottle of water from the cabinet. "Take these."

Not seeing a pot on the stove, he grunted, "Lise? Boil the water!"

"It's in the microwave. It boils faster there," she said calmly, but gave him a look, and he understood immediately how his order had sounded.

Not that she wasn't just as unhappy about every other part of this scenario too, she'd just loudly pointed out how stupid it all was. Something to be grateful for. It gave him some time to think of a way to explain to her why he owed Mateo.

"The pills won't keep this from hurting, but it should help a little."

"Shouldn't we hurry?" his friend asked, handing the bloody bottle back to him. "Doesn't it need to come out very fast to stop bleeding?"

"No. It's clotting already. Not bleeding like it was. I'm going to have to make that hole bigger, Mateo. With the knife. You want those pills to kick in first, and we need to sterilize the equipment as much as we can."

"Are you sure it's not bleeding too bad to wait?" he asked again.

"It's not bleeding much at all now, Mateo," Lise said, her voice gentle as she picked up his name and used it to connect with him. The nursing instincts must have come back when he'd made it clear he wouldn't be dissuaded.

By the time the paring knife had been in the boiled water for ten minutes, along with the other implements, the oxycodone had begun to kick in. It all came together fairly quickly.

Lise fished the tools out with metal tongs and laid them on a fresh bath towel to cool.

While the metal cooled enough to be handled, she stepped in to whisper, "We can still call an ambulance—it's not too late."

Dante took her by the shoulders and steered her away from the table, far enough that Mateo wouldn't overhear. Just tell her the bare minimum. Few details. Just get her on board.

"I know you don't understand, but he pulled my ass out of the fire once, and I owe him."

"He could die. Then what happens? How will we explain a dead man cut open on your kitchen table?!"

"He's not going to die."

Dante let go and returned to the table. "Glove up." He poured the alcohol over his hands and rolled them around, then shook them dry and squeezed his hands into the gloves.

Following his procedure, she did the same and

placed the implements far enough apart to make them easy to pick up, hard to drop.

"Mat, man. We're going to start. Try not to move. Breathe as steady as you can until I tell you otherwise, okay?"

Lise took a moment to pour some of the alcohol on paper towels and rounded the table to better reach the wounded area. "I'm trying not to get the alcohol on the actual wound while minimizing the infection risk everyone carries on their skin. If I get any on there, I'm sorry."

The blood didn't much want to wipe away with the alcohol-saturated paper towels, but she did the best she could, and apologized every time she grazed the raw flesh and paused to fan it dry with her other hand.

"Keep an eye on his pulse. If it weakens, tell me and get another BP immediately."

He needed a third hand or a second nurse when he could already hardly believe he'd dragged one nurse into this.

She'd prepared pre-torn paper towels as part of her little makeshift surgery prep, and he was glad for it. Snatching the top one, he used it to pick up the flashlight, turn it on, and shine it into the hole in Mateo's side.

But all this would've been too easy if he could've seen the bullet without cutting.

Still using the paper towel to protect his gloved hand, he stuffed the butt of the flashlight into his mouth and aimed by tilting his head, and then couldn't announce what he was doing.

He garbled around the flashlight, and Lise translated—probably only because she could anticipate him, not because she understood him.

"Cutting now, Mateo. Take a deep breath and hold it. One, two, three..."

His ribs expanded, and Lise grabbed his hand as she counted down. Dante made a quick, deep cut, his stomach lurching from the pain he knew he caused, and retracted the blade as fresh blood began to flow.

"Breathe," Lise directed, still holding his hand, but also leaning onto his shoulders with her face near his so she could look into his eyes. "You're doing really great, Mateo. Deep breaths. It's going to be okay. You know he's used to operating on brains, that's way harder than operating on bellies."

Dante didn't smile, but he wanted to. The little Truth Teller was lying to comfort. Maybe he was wearing off on her, though it would've been better for everyone if she made him a better person instead.

Putting the knife back on the towel, he pulled the extra half-inch of wound apart—causing Mateo to hiss in pain—so he could see inside, and aimed his mouth light into the bloody depths.

And he saw it—the flash of metal.

*Muchas gracias, senor.*

He sent up the prayer and noticed Lise had leaned off Mateo and put his stethoscope back into her ears. She grabbed the bulb on the pressure cuff still wrapped around Mateo's arm and began pumping.

His pulse was weakening. But stopping now would just mean that he lost blood for longer.

Pulling the wound open again, Dante reached deep with the tweezers for the bullet, but they were too short.

She pulled the stethoscope out of her ears and said, "One hundred and five over sixty."

Not great. Not as bad as it could be. He nodded, then gestured toward the wound.

"What?"

"Fashite…" he garbled.

She grabbed another paper towel to take the end of the flashlight and pulled it from his mouth.

"It's too deep for the tweezers. To get my fingers in there, I'd have to really enlarge the opening."

"What do you want me to do?"

"See if your little fingers can reach. Use middle and index."

She winced and looked at the wound. It only took her a moment to decide to do it. She changed her gloves and mimicked his method for holding the flashlight. She moved around to his left, where she could better access the wound.

He pulled the wound open and she shined the light inside, then nodded when she saw it.

"Slide them in together, slowly. Don't push it in deeper."

The look she gave him hit like a shot in the chest.

Why didn't he have his own surgery kit? This would be so much easier with forceps.

Taking a deep breath, she did as instructed. When Mateo screamed in pain, her breathing sped up and her eyebrows started to turn red. He'd seen that reddening pattern when she'd cried over baby Eli.

The opening was just about perfect for her slender fingers, so there was no seeing inside to guide her.

"The first hard thing you feel is it."

She nodded, flashlight bobbing.

"Feel it?"

Another nod from her, another cry from Mateo. He couldn't help them both at the same time.

He focused on Lise. "Open the tips of your fingers using only the second knuckles for movement. If you use your whole finger, it will flex at the opening and tear more."

She tried the motion with her left hand—the hand not shoved into Mateo's side—and then when she felt confident to do it, her eyes went a little distant as she felt her way around.

He knew the second she'd got it.

"Squeeze firmly. It'll be slippery."

Another nod.

"Deep breath, Matty. Last big pain, man."

He hoped.

When the patient complied, she drew her fingers out, and as soon as they were free, the bullet slipped from her grasp, hit the table, and bounced onto the floor.

Grabbing another fresh bath towel, he put it over the wound and applied pressure again, "Breathe. Breathe however you like now."

Then added to Lise, "Find it. See if it looks

whole, or like there are any pieces that have broken off."

She ripped her glove off, got the light from her mouth, and used it to find the bullet.

Within half a minute she had it in her hand, both of them studying it in the bright light.

"Looks a bit smashed, but I'd call that whole, wouldn't you?"

"Yes," he said, relief flooding through him. Surgery survived. Now he just had to close and keep infection at bay until Mateo healed. "Get new gloves and thread the floss onto the needle."

She went immediately to do it. The woman really was the best surgical nurse he'd ever worked with.

"How are you doing, Mat?"

"Hurts. Tired."

"After you're stitched, I'll give you another pain pill and let you sleep it off. We're almost done."

Mateo laughed, and then immediately groaned. "Hurry, *jefe.*"

It took no time to complete the few stitches the wound would need. Once he finished, Lise pumped the pressure cuff up again and added, "I laid out bandaging supplies."

* * *

Once they got Mateo doped and moved to the spare bed, Lise brought in a notepad, pen, the BP cuff, thermometer, and placed the lot on the dresser.

"I'm going to clean the back deck before the sun comes out and either bakes the blood into the paint or the neighbors see. And I may take the light around the house to make sure that it doesn't start somewhere in a trail that leads to the back door. Then I'll tackle the kitchen."

"Just do the deck and the walk around. We'll get the kitchen tomorrow. I know you're tired. You should sleep. I'll stick in here with him and keep an eye on him."

Him—who was asleep, breathing steadily and deeply, while Dante was still too high on adrenalin and stress to even think of sleeping now.

She didn't immediately leave, but stepped between his legs where he sat in the chair they'd dragged in right after putting Mateo to bed, and invited herself onto his lap.

His arms came around her and she returned the favor, giving him a warm squeeze. It was coming.

She was going to ask for those details he'd not yet decided on telling her.

She should be mad at him for taking such a risk, but it didn't look like she was. She kissed his temple and stroked her fingers through his hair. "Does he know you from the club?"

"I knew him a long time ago. He calls me *jefe* because of some illegal things we did to make cash when I was eighteen and he was fifteen."

"What kind of things?"

"Criminal things. For money." Suddenly too weary to bother lying, his mind refused to craft a more palatable alternative. He tilted his head back to look at her. "I organized, decided what posed acceptable risks, and usually kept us one step ahead." The urge to get closer welled up and he tightened his arms so he could get his face nosed in against her neck, under her hair.

"Until one time you miscalculated," she surmised.

"Mateo confessed to something they had me dead to rights for, but which we'd both done. He took full responsibility," he muttered, laying it all out without the details of the crime that had precipitated his crime toward a friend. The one that mattered to the rest of the world didn't matter to him. This was the worst part. "And I let him."

# CHAPTER ELEVEN

"What happened?"

"They let me go. He got thirty days in juvie and a year of probation. And a criminal record." He said the last part slowly, willing her to make the connection between that record and why Mateo would seek to avoid an official medical facility where they'd be under obligation to contact the police about a gunshot wound.

She nodded slowly, thinking it through. "And you were an adult at the time."

"I was an adult," he confirmed. Eighteen and always worried, always scrambling, always looking for extra money-making opportunities.

And his prison sentence would've been worse, whatever the crime. If they'd both been caught, he'd have also been contributing to the delinquency of a minor.

"My brothers don't know that either," he added, leaving unsaid the implied request that she not tell them either. "I couldn't let him go somewhere where he'd end up in jail."

She nodded. "I get it. But just because he survived the surgery…"

"I know." She didn't need to enumerate the risks of infection to him; that toxic soup was swimming through his head already. Were they at the hospital, he'd already have Mateo on IV high-dose antibiotics. They were very lucky that his bullet had more gone through the meat than the organs.

"Back then, if you'd been arrested and convicted, you wouldn't have gotten to become a doctor, would you?"

"I'm not sure. Probably not. Why are you not asking what we did? You don't want to know?"

Whatever her answer, he needed to see her when she gave it. This night had left him too mentally exhausted to think strategically.

She didn't answer right away, actually stopping to consider whether she wanted to hear the truth from him. That also seemed new.

"I do want to know, but I'm not going to ask. When you're ready, you'll tell me. And I'm going to trust it's in your past, and tonight was just…a bit of ghost chasing."

She kissed him lightly and added, "I should go

clean up before my body decides to sleep whether I'm ready or not."

"Wait." He wavered between thanking her and yelling at her for letting him drag her into illegal activities. The illegal activities part was what he should be focusing on. Suddenly, his mind sharpened.

Get her out. Give them a plausible story that she hadn't been involved in case the cops did end up involved. Minimize her exposure to it.

"Go home to the cottage tomorrow. I'll see to Mateo for the rest of the weekend, and then he should be fine to go home. But you don't need to be involved anymore."

"That's a lot for one person to do, round-the-clock nursing." She moved to stand and he held her tighter for the moment. She relaxed into his embrace again, and he knew he'd made another wrong move. He should be shoving her out the door, not clinging to her like a temperamental child. Unwrapping his arms, he grabbed her by the hips and lifted until she stood beside him.

Lise moved with him, but didn't walk out. "Are you going to sleep at all this weekend?"

"I'll stay in this chair tonight and keep a close eye on him, then spread it out tomorrow and sleep on the sofa in between." A thought sprang to mind and he couldn't ignore it. He needed those antibiotics and pain relievers for Mateo, and he couldn't leave him alone to pick them up. Picking up a prescription was less risky than her staying with Mateo in his current condition.

"You can do one thing before you go home tomorrow—pick up a couple of prescriptions at the pharmacy. I want to get him on antibiotics in the morning and he'll need a script for pain."

She finger-combed his hair back again. "Yes, and then I'll come back and help afterward. You shouldn't be by yourself in this. What if he crashes?"

"It's not your decision, Lise. This is my house and I don't want you here for this. I'll write the scripts, you can get them filled and drop them off." To make sure she listened to him, Dante pulled her hand from his hair. No distractions.

"Your house, but you keep saying this is my home now. That I should feel at home."

Mateo stirred, his medicines just not enough to keep the man out long.

Dante stood and steered her into the hallway to continue speaking. "This has nothing to do with that. This is for your good. I need to find a balance between obligations."

"Obligations?" She repeated the world, but kept her voice low even if the timbre had gone up. "Obligation to him versus obligation to me?"

That was the wrong word. He tried again, "Would desires be a better word?"

"You pretty much can't rewind away from *obligations*. But what about the chance this will come up again? In a year or ten years, when the past comes calling, will you just send me and our kids away? The cottage will be long gone by then."

It shouldn't come up again, not that he could really convince her of that right now, and it wasn't really important anyway. "Yes. Hotels will always be available. My job will be to protect my family first."

"We need to talk about this later," Lise said, the words gritting through her teeth. The splotches of pink in her otherwise abnormally pale face this morning completed the picture of how angry she was right now. "Because I'm not for you to protect. I didn't want that surgery in the kitchen, but I helped you because you needed me. I'm still helping you and I'll go away because you apparently are losing your mind with worry right now. After the fact. Since you've had a moment to weigh the dangers. But if you take this need to protect to a lying place, this isn't going to work."

She didn't wait for his response, just muttered something about blood and headed toward the veranda.

Dante returned to Mateo's room. He was still asleep. But there wouldn't be any sleep for Dante, and probably wouldn't even if he could take his eyes off Mateo long enough.

More than anything, Dante wanted his family to be safe and happy. They were generally pretty safe these days, though he sometimes had to go on the offensive to take care of problems, and the biggest threat to them now was mental and emotional well-being. And he wanted to deserve them, something he'd ceased to do a long time ago.

He'd done so much for his family that they could never know about, Lise among them. He could use a gentle and sweet woman for their good, but he couldn't justify having used her for his own good.

Helping Mateo wasn't just helping someone who had helped him, it was his way of trying to become better than he had been. Putting himself into danger for a person he didn't share blood ties with…had never happened.

He didn't want Lise to be another black mark on his soul, but that was how the situation with her felt like it was shaping up.

The instant she saw the woman appear at the end of the hallway, Lise stood from the wooden bench outside Dr. Cassie Valentino's office door.

One thing Lise could say about having a possible future family who already liked her: what other possible way could she have gotten a doctor to see her at eleven p.m. on a Friday?

"Thank you so much for doing this."

"I'm going to have to tell Rafe if this goes the way you think it's going," Cassie warned, touching her arm briefly before she unlocked the office door and led inside.

Of course she'd have to tell Rafe, they probably had a very truthful relationship. Lucky.

"Just give me some time to tell Dante first. If I am, I mean. It's possible that I'm just crazy. I pretty much feel like a basket case lately. Change stresses me out." And that wasn't even counting the kitchen surgery last week—something she was definitely not going to bring up.

They went through the office to the treatment areas. "I can do a few days without compromising my desire for an honest relationship, but let's look at your calendar before we get into all that. See what we can make of things."

Ninety minutes, a pregnancy test and a sonogram later, Lise walked out of Seaside Hospital with Cassie, unable to put the grainy black and white image of her baby away.

She was going to have a baby. She and Dante were going to be parents. And she really needed to learn to predict fertilization better after the baby came so it'd actually happen when planned next time, not a couple of weeks earlier.

She'd lied to Cassie about that, and the guilt of that lie was the only thing putting a damper on her current mood. She wanted to tell her everything that was going on. How in just under two months she'd gone from cowering behind her own walls to wanting desperately to give her trust to someone she barely knew.

"Are you okay?" Cassie asked, pausing at the juncture in the parking lot where they'd have to split up and go different directions to reach their cars.

"I'm great. Very happy. Just a bit shocked. Things with Dante…" What could she say? "He's a complicated man."

"They all are, but considering the paths most lives could've taken after what they went through… I'm pretty sure Dante can handle anything you throw at him. Even if it explodes a little at first."

"You're right." Lise nodded. This was what they both wanted. He'd just been so stiff at work this week, and after the whole Mateo thing she couldn't really blame him for being cross, but things had been different since then. It felt like he was pulling away when they had just been starting to really connect. He'd told her to stay away for a second week. When she'd asked why he'd said something about the most likely time for this situation with Mateo to backfire being within the first two weeks post-op. Somehow she wasn't supposed to be at his house if Mateo—who'd already gone home—ended up with an infection or some complications. And then there was also something about the club that didn't sound quite so ridiculous.

But she had no relationship manual to refer to, and she couldn't talk about it to this kind, generous woman because she was still bound to this double life of his. Which left Dante as the only person she could talk to, and the one person she really should talk to, but who she didn't want to talk.

"I'm going to go straight to his house and drag him out of bed if he's sleeping. I have no idea what he's up to tonight. Sometimes he ignores the world to play piano for hours..."

Cassie made some sound of understanding and that was all it took for Lise to rush forward and fling her arms around her. "I understand if you can't stay my doctor due to conflict of interest or whatever—plus it's not really your specialty, but thank you all the same."

A couple pats on the back and Cassie stepped back, "Of course. How could I pass up being the first to know if my husband's twin was going to be a daddy? And on that note, make sure to read that information I gave you about mosquitos. This is Miami. Don't let Dante have open windows and use repellent. There are some recommendations on the literature."

"Okay. I'll read it all tomorrow and pick up the spray stuff." Lise took a few steps back, looked again at her little baby bean, carefully stowed the image in her handbag where it wouldn't rumple, then called over her shoulder, "Drive safe! Don't want to upset the Valentino ecosystem."

* * *

"Lise?" Dante gave her shoulder a little shake and she immediately came awake. The last night she'd spent at Dante's house—just over a week ago—they'd been awakened by great drama. She was primed for that.

"It's okay," he reassured her, then brushed her hair out of her eyes.

Calming as quickly as she'd awakened, Lise pushed herself to a sitting position and focused her sleepy eyes on him. "Did you have a good night?"

"It was all right. Surprised to see you, though. I told you two weeks. This is one."

"I wanted to see you," she said, then frowned. "Oh, because…uh…are you sure you had an okay night?"

Dante felt a headache coming on. "It was a long night, actually. Lots of business junk I've been letting pile up."

"Did you get caught up?"

"I have to go back in tomorrow and finish."

She nodded again, glanced down the sofa to her handbag, and then looked back at him. "Did you get to play at all? I thought maybe you needed another music night with everything that happened with Mateo last week, and today was your first real day off since you spent last weekend taking care of him."

"No playing. But there was a good band up tonight. We usually have all Fridays and Saturdays booked well in advance." But he might as well have a good night since she was there. "Come to bed and make the night end on a good note."

There was another hit of hesitation, another glance at her bag, and a thoughtful pause.

"Did you want to say something?"

"No, I'm just kind of fuzzy-headed." She wiggled her fingers at her temple, then climbed to her feet and went with him.

She'd definitely been with him when he'd gone to sleep.

Dante surveyed the empty bed lit by the morning sun. A quick check of the clock confirmed it was far too early to rise on a Saturday morning.

Had she listened to him and gone home?

Unlikely.

She thought his reasoning weak and she wasn't wrong—the reason he'd given her had been weak. Because he couldn't bear to tell her the real reason.

That he'd been having second thoughts about their arrangement.

That he couldn't guarantee that he wouldn't cause risk to her because of old debts that came knocking. He couldn't think of anything else that could come, but he also knew himself and Mateo too well to think that this debt could be marked paid. If Mateo came to him with another traumatic injury or something that might cost the man his freedom, Dante was no longer certain he could turn him away.

She deserved better than a selfish man who put her into danger.

Pulling himself up, he grabbed shorts, slipped into them and shuffled through the house to find her.

"Crap!"

Her voice cut through the morning air as soon as Dante opened the bedroom door, but it sounded far away. And in pain.

He picked up speed and jogged through the house, not stopping until he found her with her back to him, standing over the kitchen sink, still muttering the same word over and over again.

"What did the sink do to you?" he asked from the doorway.

She looked over her shoulder at him, the short cotton shorts and T-shirt giving him thoughts about immediately dragging her back to bed rather than stuffing her into her car and sending her home. Her hair had been piled on her head in a sexy tangle and that did absolutely nothing to help his shifting mood.

"I like that you walk around without a shirt on all the time," she greeted with her happy, morning smile. "And don't go blaming the sink for the knife's bad behavior."

The word "knife" eclipsed the rest of her words, and pulled him urgently forward. Rounding her at the sink, he pulled her hand from the running water and watched the watery blood drip into the sink.

"I thought I'd add my DNA to the kitchen floor to complicate testing if we're ever falsely accused of a gruesome crime—more deadly than the illegal surgery, though that was pretty gruesome in a non-murderous way. Anyway, don't you kind of want to hose the floor down with that glowing CSI stuff and see how it looks? Also we should buy a new table. That one…is not food safe."

Dante listened to this chirpy morning version of Lise—a version he'd not met before—while retrieving a paper towel to staunch the blood flowing from her index finger. "It doesn't really need stitches," he said, then added, "And if they came with the glowing stuff, they'd probably only find Mateo's."

"If he ever goes missing, pray no one suspects us."

He knew that despite an early-morning knife accident, she was trying to play with him—something they hadn't done all week—but he couldn't find the humor in the situation.

By the time she'd indicted herself with the wrong pronoun, he lost his ability to smile through it. "Me. They'd suspect *me*. Not you. In fact, let's not talk about any of that ever again. Forget you were ever involved." He squeezed her injured finger, willing the blood to staunch faster so he could let go of her.

She sucked in a breath, and he could only identify it as the warning sound of an incoming fight.

"Too tight!" she grunted, but added, "Why are you freaking out?"

"Because it was illegal and even if he's not going to go talking about it, if it somehow got out, I can accept the loss of my license, but I won't accept you losing yours."

"You're not telling me this because you don't trust me not to talk about it with someone?"

"Of course not."

"But we have three…no, four secrets now. Or I do. I've no idea how many secrets you have, only that you're about to have another."

"Am I?"

She nodded, her smile returning, "I was making breakfast to surprise you."

"Lousy secret, *corazón*. I figured that out already."

"Because I have news."

He peeked under the paper towel compress and blood started to run from the slice again. "Damn."

"Told you you'd squeezed it too hard. Opened it up."

"Your fingers are too tiny and fragile. I don't know how much pressure I'm actually putting on them." He reached for her other hand and transferred it to the compress. "Apply pressure. I'll get the first-aid kit."

"Don't you want to hear my news?" she asked, stopping him before he got out of the kitchen.

"Of course I do. But I also want to get some ointment and a bandage on that cut before doing anything else." And this was all a little much for him this morning. Knife accident. Chirpy-while-injured fiancée. Him without his first sip of coffee in him yet...

And he hated surprises. Since he'd had no idea she was waiting on news, so that counted as a surprise.

Just like finding her on the sofa last night when she should've been at her home had been a surprise.

Surprise finger injury.

Surprise cheerful morning girlfriend.

Surprise breakfast for surprise news...

He snagged the kit from the bathroom and jogged back. On his way through, he found her digging in her handbag on the couch for something.

Surprise! Not where he'd left her.

"You didn't wait." And she wasn't maintaining pressure, she was shuffling through her bag.

"Yes, I did. I didn't chase you down." She pulled a piece of paper out and turned it to lay face down on the sofa beside her.

Not worth arguing about. Just get this sorted out and get some coffee.

He peeked beneath the compress again and saw only a small bead of blood on the bottom edge of the down-stroke corner, it wasn't bleeding freely any more. Good enough.

"Is the paper your news?" he asked, spreading a thin layer of antibiotic ointment over the cut.

"Finish the bandage first. I don't want to get blood on it."

"How much coffee have you had this morning?" He pulled open the bandage and carefully wrapped it around her finger. Not the right kind of bandage, but it would do for now.

"None. I'm giving up caffeine. Unless it's in chocolate."

Depositing the refuse on the table, he plucked the paper from her and flipped it over.

Testing imaging.

Black and white.

He tilted his head and felt his empty stomach turn inward.

Sonogram.

"Explain, please," he said, his voice sounding unnaturally tight to his own ears.

# CHAPTER TWELVE

SONOGRAM MEANT BABY.

The text above the image and the size of the embryo clashed with the fertility window she'd told him a couple of weeks ago.

"I was wrong about not being fertile that first night," she said, laying her newly bandaged hand over his. "I didn't mean to lie to you."

Of course she hadn't. While he'd been tap-dancing as fast as he could the past week and his entire state of confusion now necessitated more lies to her, she wouldn't lie to him.

Find something to say.

"Cassie?" he asked.

"She met me at her office at Seaside last night and we worked it out. It was the day Eli went home."

The chirpy cheer now made sense. She was genuinely happy.

"Is this what happy looks like on you?" she

asked suddenly, pulling his thoughts back to where they should've been.

"A March baby, eh?" he asked, then smiled and put the image on the table to open his arms to her.

She lunged into his arms and although she felt good against him—might always feel good against him—he could've run away.

"I love…"

*Oh, no.*

He leaned back swiftly. Pregnancy and love declaration within five minutes of one another.

Of course, it had to happen now—after it had finally become clear to him how much better she deserved.

Now he couldn't back out.

Lise saw the horror appear on Dante's face and the first words that appeared to her were lies. "I love him or her already. Don't you?"

*Lies.* Lies, because she couldn't bear that look on his face.

And it seemed to work. His brows firmed up and his mouth closed and eventually morphed into a smile. "I need coffee. And then I need to go to the jeweler."

"Today? You're going ring-shopping now?"

"I've already bought it. They had to size it and I haven't pick it up yet."

Between the speed with which he moved away and a tone in his voice, she knew he wasn't just going to get the ring. He was running away.

"It can wait. *I* can wait…"

"No. It's time for us to make this official." He disappeared off toward the bedroom—a man couldn't run away properly in his underwear.

She didn't care about the ring right now. Baby bean on the table beckoned her, and she picked up the grainy image to look some more.

"I'll be back soon. Eat some breakfast but be careful of your finger. I'll get a sleeve for you to cover it with on the way home."

He stopped in front of her, thought about something, then just as soon dismissed it and walked out.

It had taken all of eight minutes from *Look, a baby!* to *Time to go!*

But she was pretty sure the almost *I love you* was what had made him bolt.

Monday morning Show and Tell. That was what it felt like to Lise.

She had a gorgeous platinum ring with a princess-cut diamond…

She had a gorgeous fiancé with a diamond-cut rear end...

She had a secret baby growing inside her who'd done nothing so far but make her feel sleepy all the time, something her coworkers had noticed and explained as tiredness due to going at it with Dante all weekend when they should've been sleeping.

Sandy moved a mobile X-ray out of the way but positioned it close should it be needed. "Go on, tell me how he proposed."

Right. Because she should have a romantic story about that. Dante running after her aborted *I love you* definitely didn't count as a good element in those kinds of stories.

"It was more...straightforward than show-stopper," Lise said, trying to buy time as she and Sandy worked to get the surgery ready before Dante or the patient arrived.

"Details."

"Where's Marisol?" It was usually the three of them doing this job.

"Called off. Don't get off the subject. I want details!"

"There's not a lot to tell. You know Dante, he's not a flash-mob, lip-synching kind of viral video proposer. He asked, I said yes. Then he gave me this beautiful ring."

Quickly she wiped down the last surface to free her hands from the terrible burden of sterility, enabling her to fish the chain and ring that dangled from it out of her neckline to show Sandy. And after hearing the gasp every single woman who'd seen the ring had made—every woman except her—she said, "I'll show you it better after the surgery."

She didn't mention how many weeks apart each step in the proposal had been, or the various negotiations that had happened before they'd moved from one step to the next.

She *really* didn't mention how when he'd come back with her engagement ring on Saturday, he'd tossed her the velvet box while walking past, with the excuse that he had to get to the club.

And she'd maybe never tell anyone that the only person who had put the engagement ring on her finger had been herself.

She became aware of someone in the scrub bay and turned to see Dante watching them over the sinks. After stashing the ring safely back in her scrub top, she called out to him, "We're almost ready."

Then, on her way to the main door, she told Sandy, "I'll go pick up the patient. Can you re-glove and set up the instrument tray? I'll swap out the three things I'd like in different places when I get back. We'll also need the three-pin, set up at around one hundred and thirty-five degrees for a leftward head tilt."

She was starting to run out of hope, even though it was all she had going for her right now in rela-tion to Dante. The hope that one day Dante would put the ring on her finger. The hope that when they started spending time together again it would get better. Things had gotten a lot better for them between the starting weirdness of their relation-ship and Mateo's surgery. They hadn't bounced back from that, and now there was engagement weirdness on top of it. And pregnancy weirdness? It still felt like she was the only one happy about that.

Well, she and Cassie. Should've been her and Dante.

Maybe he'd come round.

Everyone wanted to see the ring, and Dante hadn't even seen it on her yet.

Saturday, after he'd given it to her, he'd spent the

rest of the day—well, into the wee hours—at the club, first doing paperwork and then just listening. He'd stayed gone long enough for her to go home. Cowardly. And confusing. And all Dante had to explain it to himself was unease with her since Mateo.

Had she told people she was pregnant along with the news of their engagement?

Every time he tried to think about the two of them—or the three of them—it was like there were bees in his head. Angry bees. Some mix of guilt and fear. The guilt part he understood, he'd summoned her into a situation that was dangerous for her, simply because he'd wanted something.

Anger was there too. It went along with the guilt—he was still angry with himself for putting her into danger. But there was something else, and fear was as close as he could come to naming it. Which should be the first step in figuring out how to fix it.

Finding out she was pregnant while still trying to sort himself out only complicated their situation.

The big door opened and Lise wheeled the patient in on his hospital bed. Several other members of the team trailed in behind her and they moved him over to the table and removed the big bed.

Finishing his scrub, he was gowned and went to speak with his patient as the anesthesiologist moved in and started setting up different medicines for the IV.

"Good morning, Mr. Morris. Can you tell me what we're doing today?"

"The tumor ain't rotted my brain yet, Doc. We're taking it out, I hope."

Dante smiled at the older man. "I hope so too. Don't worry, you're in good hands. My team's the best around."

The first push of sedative hit in the next moment, and their patient's eyes fell shut.

Lise buzzed out of the scrub bay—he could tell and he had his back to her. In the last few weeks he'd learned to identify her by her walk, and even sometimes when she was very quiet he could tell when she'd come near him.

*Wonder if that'd show up on an MRI?*

Time to get it together. Stop thinking about the incomprehensible moodiness he'd been feeling ever since he'd got exactly what he wanted.

The anesthesiologist indicated Mr. Morris had

reached the right level of unconsciousness. Time to begin.

Pretend it was three months ago, don't focus on what happened three days ago.

"Bradshaw." He called her by her last name—something he'd stopped doing since they'd been together. It helped him focus.

"Yes, Dr. Valentino?"

He started issuing orders, starting with a call for the clippers to come out.

Without a word she got the razor from a drawer beside the table and turned it on but waited for him to indicate precisely where he wanted the head shaved.

Bradshaw.

*Bradshaw.*

Valentino. Soon…

It was starting to feel like they populated half the city.

He could understand why she'd gone to Cassie for this, but the idea of his sister-in-law ministering to his wife and child set current sizzling over his head and down his spine.

She wasn't even an OB/GYN. And Lise would go to a better hospital. Seaside was okay, but Buena Vista had better facilities.

Once it was all out in the open—engagement, pregnancy—she could go to an OB within the facility.

Trimming done, Lise took the next step on her own, slathering an antiseptic wash over the man's head and part of the way down his face, painting him a strange shade of blue-green.

The sterile drapes came next, and she offered the scalpel he preferred to start with.

After the skin incision was made, the drill was immediately in his hand before he asked.

A quick inspection of the bit size she'd chosen and he saw it was the size he'd have requested.

Inside the upper right parietal quadrant, he carefully bored a hole and handed the drill back. The craniotomy came next.

She was the best damned surgical nurse he'd ever worked with. Maybe that was part of the draw. She anticipated his needs in the OR, she even anticipated them in bed. The more time they spent together outside those two activities, the more she seemed to see. She knew about the club. She knew he'd engaged in illegal activities to provide for his family as a young man. He'd almost told her what he and Mateo had been up to when they'd been busted years ago. Stupid instinct, but she made that open manner of living look so easy. What she didn't realize was that some people—people like him—couldn't do that without losing everything.

When she learned enough, she'd eventually have to leave him. She'd already started to pick up on that too—why else would she plainly state that she wasn't going to ask what they'd done that meant Mateo had wound up in juvie? Self-preservation. She didn't want it to factor in.

They'd finally finished the craniotomy to expose the dura covering the brain.

"It's discolored," she whispered, those two words letting him know she knew exactly what they were going to find.

Malignancy. They'd known they were going after a meningioma, but so few of those tumors were ever malignant…

All he did was nod, not diagnosing aloud before he confirmed it with his own eyes.

Time for the finer instruments.

She raised a pole with the loops on it that would make it easier to see what he was doing when he got in there right up against the delicate organ.

They'd been in the OR for a couple of hours,

and in a few more he'd have to find the family and deliver bad news.

Which was why Valentinos shouldn't treat other Valentinos. If anything went wrong...

The violence that rose in him at the idea of something happening to Lise made his hand twitch. She'd been just about to place his preferred bipolar forceps in his hand—so he'd been away from the patient at the time—but that kind of undesired, uncontrolled movement spawned by a fleeting idea that something could happen to her? He'd only ever had that stomach-plummeting sensation from fear when thinking of family and losing them.

And now he had it about Lise.

He waited a moment, not trusting his hand or really any part of his body for the moment.

She shifted at his side, and he looked down at her, meeting her concerned eyes. There was a connection between them and it comforted him. It steadied him.

Even though he was the biggest danger to her.

The Inferno doormen didn't know her, but Lise had money and a valid ID showing her to be of drinking age. She also had a ring on her finger that should've let her through the back, but she paid the cover anyway.

Dante wasn't answering her calls anymore.

He hadn't spent any time with her outside of surgery since he'd flung the engagement ring at her a week ago.

Every step she took into the club, her insides shook. The past three days, all the morning sickness she hadn't been having had hit at once. If she threw up on him, he had it coming.

Dante didn't know any of that because after Monday's grueling craniotomy and tumor removal, he'd "loaned" her back to the hospital. No explanation, he'd just gotten her out of his sight, whether she wanted to go or not.

It hadn't taken her that long to work out what was going on. He'd changed his mind, he just hadn't bothered to tell her about it.

What she didn't know was whether he'd changed his mind before or after she'd told him about the baby. The night before, when he'd found her asleep on the sofa, things had been really good. They'd both wanted a family, it had been the driving force of their coming together, so her pregnancy didn't feel like a valid reason for him to lose it like this.

If he was backing out now, he could darn well give her an explanation.

"Hey," she called, and flagged down the server who'd supplied her with a steady mojito stream that first night.

It took some persuading and flashing her ring as proof, but she found herself standing before Dante's office door for what felt like an hour. She was only certain time was still moving because of the waves of nausea hitting her.

This could go one of two ways, she figured. She could just leave him without being willing to try again. Or she could confront him and he could realize that this was all flaming out, and change.

Actually letting those words take shape in her head made her want to run away.

No. She didn't need to run, she'd done nothing wrong—except for maybe overlooking warning signs for far too long. That had been wrong, and stupid, and a rookie error.

But he'd talk to her first—she deserved that.

After? She didn't want to think about after.

She was strong. Knew how to adapt. She could be enough for this child. None of her plans ever went off without hitches, and she always muddled through.

"Just do it," she whispered under her breath, stopping the mental pep talk.

*It's better to know.*

It *was* better to know. The truth may not always be easy or pretty, but it was healthier.

Dropping her hand onto the knob, she pushed her way right in.

Dante's office looked precisely like as she'd pictured: another uncomfortable sofa—which Dante currently lay on with a tumbler of booze in one hand—plain walls, file cabinets, a heavy wooden desk, and a few musical instruments strewn about.

He preferred *this* to being with her?

Another wave of nausea hit, stronger than the others. She took two steps to a trash can and bent over it, ready for another wave to turn her inside out.

There would be no convincing him or changing him.

"Lise?" He said her name but didn't come to help her, despite her obvious distress,

Once more her stomach lurched, but she made herself stand up straight.

"You do remember me, I see."

She'd practiced the things to say all day long, but she'd never discovered a magic order, a manner, or the right *something* that would make Imaginary Dante react in a way that saved their little family.

Even Imaginary Dante refused to play along anymore.

"Much as I drink, I do still remember you."

"So this is it, then?" she asked, breathing slowly and deeply as her body seemed ready to try and rid her of her supper. Despite the difficulty that came with talking in this condition, she turned her head to look at him. "This is how your marriage scheme ends? With you hiding in a bar, drinking, and me trying to interpret your silence every hour of the day, trying to find some way to make sense of it?"

"Just get to what you wanted to say," Dante said, and she could see he wasn't drunk—he watched her like a doctor, ready to help, though he never made any move toward her.

"I deserve to know why." She cried the words, shaking her head. "You've been different since Mateo. Why? Did he die and you decided not to tell me so I couldn't be involved?"

"He's alive," Dante muttered, and took another drink of the amber liquid. "That's not what you want to do here. You want to yell, but it won't change anything. You'll still be angry in the end. Trust me."

"Why in the name of all that's holy would I trust you over anything?"

"Good point."

"That's it? Good point? That's all you're going to say?"

Dante plowed a hand through his hair. "What else is there? You're hurt but you originally wanted to be a single parent. You know you can do it alone."

"So you're rejecting both of us? Let me guess, she'll be born outside wedlock, so she won't be a real Valentino, much like your brothers' wives."

"I never said that. But us splitting up is the right decision. You raising the baby is the right decision. I'll provide financially anything either of you need, but we can't raise this child together."

"You still haven't said why. You don't want me now. I get it. I don't know what I did. And the funny thing is that this was after I discovered your weakness: you can't lie during sex. But I can't even bring that kryptonite into play with you avoiding me."

"You don't know every time I lie to you, Lise.

Did you work out that I manipulated you into agreeing to this hare-brained scheme?"

"How did you do that? With sex? Conversation? Spending time with me? That's not manipulation, it's a relationship."

"I handed you a bloody, traumatized baby the week after I learned that you had no family and it scared you to think about what might happen to your children if something happened to you. So I made that happen, and counted on your goodness to take you exactly where I wanted you to go."

The words he said made sense as words, but they still didn't want to settle into a pattern she could understand. "You made the accident happen?"

"I saw Eli as an opportunity and handed him to you. Then it was just a matter of saying the right thing when you came to me heartbroken over him."

"You're lying. You wouldn't do that. No one would do that!" She felt the food rising again.

"Mateo and I—"

"No!" she yelled. "Don't you say another word."

"I saw a chance to unburden myself—to take some of the red out of my books with Mateo—

and I used you without even a fleeting thought for your welfare."

She spun on heel and began pacing his office, her knees itching with the desire to run, and every piece of her heart wanting to plug her ears and not listen.

"I picked you and decided to marry to keep my family from worrying about me. That—keeping up appearances—was ninety-seven percent of my reasoning."

"Was the other three percent sex?"

"We have outstanding chemistry."

Lise stopped pacing in front of him and held out her left hand, fingers extended, flashing the engagement ring weighing down her third finger.

"What?"

"Take it back. I don't even know why you gave it to me to start with."

She'd put it on every time, but if he took it off once, maybe she'd be able to accept this as done, and this was not simply some kind of horrible misunderstanding.

And maybe he'd really realize what he was doing by her making him take it off her finger, because that stupid thought continued to rattle around in her mind. She'd always known she shouldn't trust him, but he'd made her, and now she wanted to. She wanted to throw him a lifeline, or just a darned hint, and if nothing else, the ring was the best hint she had to offer.

Dante looked at her hand, unmoving, while her heart and stomach ganged up on her.

After a tense moment his voice lost any emotion again, and he said, "Keep it."

A bitter laugh tore from her, "I never wanted it. I only demanded it as a way to bide time before telling anyone about us. Because I was afraid of this." She wrenched the ring violently from her finger and dropped it straight into his tumbler of booze.

He flinched back then, and slammed the glass onto the nearest table.

"I knew this could never work out, but I still wanted it to. Enough that I walked right toward the cliffs, telling myself that you deserved the benefit of the doubt."

She felt herself breathing faster, trying not to vomit.

*Just wrap it up.*

He'd probably only lie to her if she actually got an explanation from him anyway. *Finish it.*

"Transfer me back to the hospital permanently,

would you? Off Neurosurgery—any surgical unit will work. Just do it fast, or Monday I'm quitting, and you know how important it is for a single parent to have a stable job." She marched for the door, but stopped and turned midway to come back to him, digging keys, a garage door opener, and her sonogram image from her bag. She dropped them on the sofa beside him.

"I'm no good for you, Lise. You'll see. This is for the best. I know you'll be a good mother."

"Shut up, Dante. Crawl back into your bottle and your pretend life. Or, you know, talk to someone you trust—someone clearly not me, ironically. And if no such person exists, get a dog. Because whatever it is that's wrong with you...it's a cancer."

Monday morning Lise reported to her first day as a regular RN on the general surgery floor at Seaside Hospital. Having contacts at each hospital had facilitated a quick transfer. At least here she could visit Cassie and Saoirse. Kiri would've no doubt been kind to her had she stayed at Buena Vista, but meeting Dante would always have been a possibility around the next corner. The other Valentinos would be easier to run into.

She wouldn't be in surgery for the foreseeable future, until she got a new surgical nurse position. If she decided to do that.

It wasn't the same kind of high-technology facility that she was used to at Buena Vista, but Kiri's help had gotten her out of Dante's territory, which was worth the step down in skill and pay.

Because Dante had taken time off and she was his employee, there weren't any laws being violated by her not giving two weeks' notice. Now, if she could just avoid the brothers who roamed these halls, she might make it through this.

That plan had lasted until Wednesday afternoon when she'd come across Santiago and Saoirse in Emergency, and the pregnant Irish woman had cornered her to check on her.

"I can't talk about this," Lise said immediately. "He's not my business anymore. He doesn't want us around, so I just needed to be out of Buena Vista. Here, the only people who'll know my story aren't likely to put it on the rumor mill."

Saoirse touched her arm and Lise shrugged

back. "Please don't be kind to me right now, I'll cry. It's not a good thing to do at a new job."

"If you need anything, even if you two aren't together anymore, that baby is still family and you have every right to hold onto that. Keep in touch, and if you do need anything you call me and Santi first. You're always welcome at our house."

"Dante wouldn't be happy."

"So what? He won't be there. And he's—"

"On vacation," Lise finished up. "I heard. Caribbean or somewhere."

"He didn't go on vacation. He's just not answering phone calls or speaking to anyone. Rafe went over to make sure he wasn't dead, and got a bottle chucked at his head. We only found out you guys had split after you called Kiri."

So he was self-medicating with booze. What reason did *he* have to be upset? He didn't want *them*.

"I'll think about it. I still have two hours left on my shift—don't want to lose my job, so I'd better go."

Working was preferable to speaking with his lovely family. That led to thinking about him, and that just wouldn't work for her right now.

Working was much better.

She should put her CV in at other local hospitals to see if she could get a surgical nurse position somewhere that she didn't have to run into his family.

Maybe she should aim for Ft. Lauderdale. Or Anchorage.

Lise stepped into the bodega's back room on inventory night.

"I'm giving him some space. I don't like being target practice." Rafe's voice boomed like a wall that surrounded them and kept her frozen at the door.

She paused at the door, giving them an opening to tell her to leave.

They all quieted and turned to look at her, but no one ordered her to go.

"I can see this time. Dark sunglasses outside means less sun-blindness when I come into this dark room."

"He's not here, Lise," Alejandro said, his voice gentle.

"Neither are the other Valentinos, it looks like. Everyone okay?"

"They're fine. At home, cooking something,"

Santiago answered, then turned the question back on her. "Are you okay?"

She wasn't going to lie to him, but she also didn't think she should just answer that question truthfully. "I'm here to count. I had a talk with your lovely wife and she reminded me of something important."

"What's that?"

She took the fourth clipboard ledger with pen, and went to the fourth area to start looking for the applicable items. "That I should maintain contact with the family of my child. I'm not here to talk about Dante, and only because he's not here. I don't have any family of my own. And it's an immense comfort to me to keep in mind that one of you could take and raise my baby if something ever happened to me. So that's why…I'm here."

She stumbled over the last bit, and felt even more nervous than she sounded, trying to put the words together.

"Of course we would do that," Rafe said, his words gruff. "We can even have it put into writing if you wish. If it'd give you peace of mind."

She nodded quickly. "It would. Thank you. I appreciate that a lot. I don't know the gender yet, or if that matters to who might want to do the raising. Just discuss amongst yourselves and let me know, and I'll get papers drawn up. And thank you again."

"Gender doesn't matter. And use me and Cassandra. We'll gladly sign. And you're using insect repellent, right? She told you to do that."

"Religiously. Thank you for that too."

The door rocked open and Dante trundled in, a flask in one hand.

Lise froze, then felt herself shrinking, trying to hide behind the flats of canned goods.

She didn't want him to see her. If Saoirse hadn't said that he was avoiding everyone, she would've just called!

Could she get to the store door and out that way to avoid going past him?

He began speaking in loud and somewhat slurred Spanish, and she understood nothing he said. She heard her own heart beating in her ears, deafening.

The rest of the room had gone quiet too, and Dante finally picked up on it. He paused, cocked his head to the side, and then turned and looked straight at Lise.

Her pulse shot up to speeds high enough to make her feel light-headed.

Carefully, she laid down the clipboard and reached for her purse. Slow and easy, as if moving in front of a wild, angry animal.

"*Por que* are you *aquí*?" He shouted the Spanglish question at her, and she knew those words.

"I was just here to..." Her thundering heart wasn't about fear, she realized. She was angry. Just angry right now. "I was asking for volunteers to raise your child in case something happens to me. Is that all right with you? What are *you* doing here? Really think you can count helpfully when you're seeing double?"

Dante groaned loudly and paced away from her. Again the language switches happened, back and forth, and at a speed and volume that only let her know one thing: he wasn't sad any more, he was angry, too. Angry! The nerve of that man!

And not a damned bit of it made sense.

There was something about ruining his life, and something else about his club.

She could've laughed, only she didn't know if the brothers would pick up on it or not. She also really could've enjoyed beaning him on the head with a can of tomatillos, but he was doing a good enough job of killing brain cells without her helping.

"I was here first, doofus. You can't stalk someone by going somewhere first when you never expected them to show up. And? Don't worry, I'm leaving anyway. I'm going to go to this club I heard of, The Inferno? See if I can't find an idiotic musician to sleep with!"

Dante opened his mouth and then closed it again.

Clearly, she could only out-yell him when he was drunk out of his mind and she couldn't understand most of what he said.

The last thing she heard from inside was Rafe asking, "What club are you talking about? You own a club?"

Dante watched through bleary eyes as Lise left. Then Rafe was saying something he couldn't work out.

Club?

He wasn't sober enough for this conversation. Was it always going to hurt like this?

Turning, he headed for the door and got it cracked open before an arm came around his neck and dragged him back inside.

When Rafe released him, all three of his brothers blocked his path and shoved him down onto one of the crates.

"What's going on with you? You fall for her, bring her to meet us, get her pregnant, then dump her?" Rafe spat out one question after another. And what could Dante say? Yes. He'd done those things.

"But you don't want to feel broken up, so you crawled into a bottle of bourbon?" Alejandro asked. His youngest brother thought he knew best now.

"Someone get coffee going," Rafe said, snagging Dante's bottle and handing it to Santiago as he dragged a chair over to sit in front of him. "Spill it. If there's a problem, we'll work out how to fix it."

"I don't need to rely on you to make my decisions again," Dante muttered, and suddenly his head started to throb. He leaned forward and propped his elbows on his knees, then dropped his head into his hands.

"What decisions do I make for you usually?"

He couldn't answer that. He wouldn't.

"Focus," Rafe said, punching him on the shoulder.

Dante swayed back, his still present anger bubbling up again. "Don't push me, Rafe."

"I don't want to make decisions for you. I don't

often like making them for myself. What decisions do I make?" Another clap to his shoulder sent him swaying back.

"You know what decision you had to make for me!"

# CHAPTER THIRTEEN

LISE HEARD THE knock at her front door and jogged to answer it. "Come on, courier..."

It had been a week since the big explosion at the bodega, and she hadn't heard a peep from a single Valentino, something she tried very hard not to think about. After the way she'd had a screaming match with their drunken brother, they probably thought she was at least a little unhinged. But hopefully Rafe and Cassie would still sign the agreement that she'd spoken to them about before things had all gone spiraling out of control.

Flinging the door open, she froze at the sight of Dante standing on her front step. Sober and clean, wearing a suit—all three pieces. Of course he'd come when she was wearing yoga pants and had her hair in a messy ponytail on top of her head.

Before either of them spoke, he held out a folio toward her.

Papers. Fear flared to life deep in her belly.

"What's this?" She didn't take it.

"Legal documents."

Lise wordlessly turned and darted back inside. As soon as her hand found the door, she slammed it with all her might!

A howl of pain erupted from the other side and she looked down to see one shiny shoe wedged between the door and frame.

"Go away, Dante. You cannot have this baby! I don't care what legal documents you have in your hand. This child is mine. You said you don't want it, and it's in my body, and you can just go to hell!"

"They're not mine. A courier brought them." He grunted, then flattened his hand against the door and pushed it open enough to get his body wedged into the gap. "Here. Were you expecting documents? I'm guessing the arrangement with Rafe and Cassie?"

She eyed the man half inside her house and then the folio again. "Yes. Why did the courier give it to you?"

"Because I said I was going in."

"And he just believed you?"

He shrugged.

She snatched the thing from his hand and then

tossed it onto the floor a short distance away so she didn't have to let go of her door. "What do you want, then?"

Whatever he said, she knew better than to take his word. Even asking for clarification seemed like an exercise in futility. And heartache. Just because she hadn't loved him long didn't mean she could get over him fast. Seeing him standing there, beautiful temptation, even knowing how things always went... hurt.

"I'm here to beg for your forgiveness," he said, mouth grim. "I actually tried to prepare my apology ahead of time, but—"

"Fine. You're forgiven, now go away," she said, placing one hand against his upper arm and shoving to get him out before that ache she felt when she even thought about him made her stupid again. "Go home. Or wherever else you want to be."

"I want to be here."

"Well, I'm done with your games and your manipulations. I'm done dancing like a puppet on your strings. So find somewhere else you want to be. And get out of my house." She shoved again, in case he really was that thick that he didn't get her request to go away.

Dante sighed and stepped through the door to stand just on the outside of it so it could be closed. "Please, just hear me out, and then if you want me to go, I'll go. But things are different. I'm different."

Lise slammed the door, and took her time turning all the locks and applying the chain. She then stormed over to the sofa and crawled onto it, having furniture that practically hugged her had become something she needed more and more lately.

Dante took his jacket off. It was late August in Miami, and it was hot. The black jacket was only making him more miserable. Stepping off the top step, he dropped down to sit on the small concrete porch and waited, the knot in his gut tightening with every baking second.

Twenty minutes later, the little door on the brass mail slot popped open and Lise called through it. "You have to leave if I ask, it's the law. I'll call the cops, Dante! See how well you can keep up appearances if you get arrested!"

"That might be kind of you. It's really hot out here, and this suit is wool."

He may have come here to talk to her, but he

couldn't stay much longer if he didn't get inside or a gallon of water to drink soon.

"A good reason to get into your air-conditioned car."

He tilted his head and looked into the mail slot, and saw her peeking at him. "If I leave, I'll just come back later. I have to. I'm not…ready to give up on you," he said, knowing even as he said the words that he'd never be ready to give up on her. It was only recently that he'd realized he'd all but given up on himself years ago. "If you hear me out and you still want nothing to do with me, I will understand. I'll respect your wishes. I know you have no reason to trust me."

"That's right, I don't."

"I told them about the club."

"Yes, in all your drunken shouting, you mentioned the club. And then as I was leaving, they questioned you about it. You said what?"

"That I owned it, that I played in a band there, and that I'd kept it from every single person who knew me as a surgeon, except Fate had sent you to me, so you were the only one who knew."

The door on the slot closed and his head hung forward. "That wasn't all I told them. It was the start."

He heard several of the locks tumble and stood up, but when she opened the door, the chain was still there. He could see her now, though, and he could stand close enough to the house to get a little of the shade cast by the eaves.

"So now I'm supposed to what?"

"Nothing. There's a lot more. I told them a lot. I even told them the reason I kept it hidden."

"Sanctuary?"

"Because it felt like a gateway place to my past, and the things I've done that I had to keep them from knowing."

She made a disgruntled sound, the door slammed again, but then the chain moved and she opened the door fully. "If I ask you to leave, you have to go. Don't make me push you out the door again. I'm not kidding, I will call the police."

Hope surged in him, but he knew better than to get too excited. Nodding, he grabbed his jacket off the railing, and stepped into the cool little cottage.

"I'll get you a drink."

A moment later she came back with ice water, set it on a coaster on the table, and moved to stand across the room from him.

He lifted the glass and drank tall the contents

down in one go, leaving only tinkling ice at the bottom. "It's a long story, *cora*—"

"Don't call me that."

He nodded again and peeled his vest off and rolled up his shirtsleeves. "Please, sit. It's going to take a while."

Lise reached up to pull her hairband out, dropping it on the coffee table as she came round to sit on the couch, and dug her fingers into her hair to massage her scalp.

"Headache?"

"Yes."

He nodded, but didn't offer treatment. Even though he wanted to.

"I'm not sure what order to do this in, so I'm probably going to bounce around a lot." He grabbed the coffee table and scooted it out another couple feet so he could sit on the edge and face her but not be close enough to crowd her.

"Do whatever you like. You said you weren't leaving until you said your piece, so…"

"The thing is, I did those things to you. I put you into a night of horror and grief with baby Eli, though I didn't think it would be that long. I thought a couple of hours, no big deal…but then you'd see my argument without me making it over and over and over and you not listening."

"I always listened. But you have an agenda, Dante. Even right now you have an agenda. I don't know what it is. How about you start there?"

He felt his stomach curdle, took a deep breath and nodded. "My agenda is to make you understand that I love you, and that I'm a complete monster sometimes, and that I want to be with you, and I want to do better. And I want you. I just want you. I want our baby. I want you both. I love you both."

Lise stopped rubbing her fingertips into her tense scalp, feeling a headache starting.

He didn't sound polished at all, he always sounded polished. "Those sound like very nice words. Tell me why I'm supposed to believe them."

"When the shootings happened, I lost my mind. Mom died at the scene. Alejandro was dying, and the neurosurgeon at the hospital said they could get the bullet out and save my dad's life. And I believed it. I needed to believe it, so I just did. But things didn't go that way. I don't know what he did wrong—all I know is after the surgery Dad was brain dead, but the rest of his body was in good shape. No matter how smart I was, I couldn't accept the idea that the doctor who'd been so sure, who I'd put my faith in, was wrong. I thought Dad would wake up at any time and he'd be okay."

He'd never talked that openly with her, and she felt the remains of memories in his voice, saw it in his eyes, and wanted to believe, but she wasn't there yet. "How did you figure it out?"

"I didn't. The surgeons were telling us that we had to make the decision on whether to give Dad's heart to Alejandro, but I still couldn't believe that he wasn't just going to wake up. So even though my little brother needed that heart, and even though I knew my father would want him to have it, it felt like murder to me. So I didn't help. I didn't support Rafe. I was supposed to be his partner in it since we were the oldest, but I was useless." He shook his head and his eyes were glassy. It took him a moment to swallow it down.

She wanted to reach for him. And it sucked. He was a gifted liar, this could all be just like it had been with Eli, designed to pull her in.

"So Rafe signed the papers. I lost it. I said some nasty things to him, and I went to sit with my dad as life support was terminated. And then he was gone, and they took him to surgery and harvested his heart. And they took Alejandro—who was the skinniest ten-year-old you ever saw—and cut open his chest and put my dad's heart into him. It took me a few days to accept it. It might have taken longer. I don't know when I accepted that he'd been gone right after the surgery, my dad. I accepted earlier that he'd have wanted us to make that call for our brother. I accepted that a lot earlier than I accepted that it wasn't also a murder."

She watched his eyes, feeling the burn that set her vision shimmering, mirroring the dampness in his dark brown eyes. She didn't look away, but have something to say? That wasn't in her either yet.

"My brothers forgave me a long time ago."

"Forgave what?"

"How entirely I let my family down. How entirely I let my twin down, and my youngest brother—someone my father would've wanted me to protect. So Rafe carried that decision on his own. And I've…spent the last eighteen years trying to fix it."

They sniffed at the same time, and Dante leaned over for his jacket, fished around in the inside pocket and handed his handkerchief to her, swiping his eyes with his palm afterward.

"How do you fix that? Apologizing?"

He shook his head. "By providing. By making sure that the rent got paid and the water and we had food and whatever else that the social workers might object to us lacking when they came to check and make sure we were taking good care of Alejandro. Everyone pitched in to help us get by—Santi ran the bodega mostly by himself. Rafe and I had part-time jobs and we all had school. And I had my criminal endeavors."

Lise wiped her eyes with the hanky and finally pulled her gaze away, focusing on the crisp, folded linen. "Are you going to tell me what you and Mateo did?"

"I'll tell you anything you want to know, Lise. Anything."

The gruff, raw sincerity in his voice pulled her eyes back to him, and made the tears fall faster.

"We stole things. Fancied ourselves Robin Hoods, but the poor we gave to were us. We ran poker games twice a week, cheated, and got in a number of violent altercations when our customers figured it out and objected. I've destroyed property—cars, windows in houses. I conned older rich ladies who stayed at the places where

I played piano. I had no shame. Have... Had...I guess I do have it now."

"What are you ashamed of?"

"I pushed you away because I realized that I still have that instinct in me to protect, no matter what the cost. I started to realize it that night of Mateo's surgery, and afterward I was so angry with myself for letting you help. And I realized it fully during our last surgery, when I was panicking and knew you loved me, but didn't think I deserved it. I don't..." He stopped stumbling along and rubbed the back of his neck.

"You don't have to say any more if you don't want to. I know this is hurting you."

"I need you to understand. I have to say it." He took a breath and tried again. "In that surgery, I thought about losing you and the baby, or even just you...and I felt anger and violence in me like I've never felt. I almost dropped the forceps you handed me."

"Your hand twitched."

He nodded. "That was the realization I've done bad things—mostly the worst ones were a long time ago—to look out for my family. But I couldn't think of one thing I wouldn't do to protect you. I think, where you're concerned, I could do much worse than I've done for my siblings. That's not the kind of man you deserve. That's not the kind of man I want to be, even if you kick me out after this and never look back. I want to be what I made you see. So I got really drunk for a couple of weeks, and I hurt you. And, honestly, I don't even know how to apologize for that. I am sorry. I know that you deserve better."

"Did you tell Rafe you were sorry?"

He nodded, emotion overwhelming him so that he slid onto the floor in front of her and buried his face in her lap.

"Did he forgive you?"

"He said he didn't have to." His voice had grown hoarse, and when he looked up at her, misery saturated his bloodshot eyes. She stroked her fingers over his eyes to brush away the wetness.

"Do you believe him?"

He shook his head, the torture in his face making her own tears flow freely down her cheeks.

"If I tell you I forgive you, will you believe me?"

A helpless shake of his head and he whispered, "I don't know. I'd want to, though."

"I forgive you." She leaned forward, stroking his cheeks to tilt his head back, her fingers disappearing in his hair to hold on as she brushed the gentlest kiss over his brow, over his cheeks and, finally, his lips.

The first touch of her lips to his and a gravelly, ragged sound scratched up his throat, like that of a wounded animal, as his arms dove around her hips to pull her to him. In one powerful lift, he picked her up to roll gently onto the carpet with him.

Though she could see how it cost him, he moved over her slowly, giving her time to push him away, to say no, to say she hated him, to take it all back. That uncertainty she'd felt for months was unconcealed in his eyes.

Hooking her thumbs under the waistband of her pants and panties, she tugged them off, and once the material flew off her kicking feet she reached for his belt.

"You want to?" he said, looking into her eyes as if he couldn't quite believe his luck.

"Yes. I always want you, but do you know the other reason?"

It took him a moment, but slowly he nodded. "Because you trust me when I'm inside you. Because you know I can see you when I'm inside you, and I want you to believe what I'm telling you. That I can see the truth in your eyes, and that I know you.

"Believe that you know me," he whispered the correction, but accepted her invitation, wrapping her legs around him and thrusting into her as far as their bodies would allow, then set the rhythm of a man who'd never believed he'd feel pleasure, or comfort, or love again.

"So *you* can believe *me* when I tell you that I can still love you." Pulling her legs back, she pressed against the floor and he rolled with her so that she straddled him and stopped him moving.

"Oh, please, love. I need…"

"Wait."

She sat up and caught his hands as he reached for her hips, his breathing labored, the whole of him silently begging for her to free him, to save him.

He sat up and when she let go of his arms he wrapped them around her and just held on.

"Do you believe me?" She started to move, tilting his head up to look at her. "Do you know that you're worthy of my love? That you deserve me and our child? Our family?"

He shook his head, but his whole body shook too, as if in the grip of a terrible fever.

"What can I say that will help you believe me?"

"I don't know," he answered immediately, then groaned as she began to move again, tilting and grinding her hips down on him.

"Do you believe I'm a good person?"

"Yes."

She kept her movement slow even as sweat broke out across his brow.

*"Por favor, querida..."*

She tilted his head back again so she could look into his eyes. Spanish came with his passion. *"Por favor, querido,"* she repeated back. *"Creas a me?"*

Her Spanish really wasn't good.

He grinned a little through pain as she held him on the cusp of climax and wouldn't let him cross over.

"I'm trying to believe," he said in English.

She pressed against his shoulders until he lay back, and she went with him. "I wouldn't lie to you."

He nodded, his hands to her hips to grip her, his body shaking.

"Do you trust me?"

A nod was all he could muster, but his eyes still looked worried. Scared.

Her own body slowed down faster than his did,

and it became less difficult to be still with him, though she made sure to rotate her hips frequently enough to keep him at that exhausting edge.

"Do you think I would make the right decision in those iffy situations?"

He nodded again, his fingers biting into her hips as he groaned, still trying hard to do what she wanted.

"Then all you have to do is tell me when you get those bad feelings and we'll figure a way out."

*"Te necesito."*

"Say yes." She stroked his damp hair back from his face. "I'm not ready to give up on you."

He shook his head, not managing words again. He looked away from her until she leaned over him, close enough that their warm, moist breath mingled even in the fast, furious breathing ripped from them.

"You're a good man, Dante. You're worthy of us, of your family, of your siblings already. You can love your brothers' wives as your sisters and not risk committing additional sins for them. Do you believe me?"

His hands finally left her hips and slid up her back so he could pull her tight against him, and she felt the urgency to finish fading in him, but he still couldn't get close enough to her.

*"Voy a creer lo que me dices que crea,"* he whimpered against her throat.

"I don't know what that means," she whispered, finger-combing his hair again.

"I'll believe what you tell me to believe." He took control then and rolled her onto her back until he was settled against her and able to look her in the eye. "I'll work on it. I won't fail you. I won't fail you or the baby…however many we have. I keep my promises, Lise."

He settled into the rhythm she'd been withholding from them both, and soon she felt tears on her cheeks at the moment of climax.

Warmth once again seemed to settle into her bones, comforting and protected.

"Tell me what to believe," he asked again, and leaned up to look at her.

The ache that had set up in her breast eased, and she couldn't resist playing with him. "You should believe that beach weddings are the very best."

Dante tilted his head, but slowly grinned at her. "I should?"

"Mmm-hmm," she said, tugging his mouth back to hers for a soft, loving little smooch.

Sweetness flowed between them, and he looked her in the eye again. "Anything else?"

"That women who have massive round bellies are beautiful, and that you'll love the way I look even if my breasts swell up until I look like one of those photos of plastic surgery gone awry."

"That one's easy." He smiled finally, tiredly, then rolled with her again until she was stretched out on his chest and his arms came around her, nothing overtly sexual in the touches, just the touch of a man who couldn't believe his fortune. "Anything else?"

"That I love you and know you're a good man. I wouldn't stay with you, no matter how much I love you, if I thought you would be a danger to our baby. Do you believe me?" Her voice cracked. It was the last, the playful humor of moments before gone.

"Always."

And she knew it was true. Even without looking at him. Even without feeling it except when he let his guard down in moments of passion, it swam up at her like truth and she knew it.

Even if it took him the rest of his life to accept her estimation of his goodness and worth, she'd stay beside him, always reminding him.

And probably arguing about random inconsequential things.

Everyone needed a hobby.

* * * * *

*We hope you enjoyed the final story in the*
HOT LATIN DOCS *quartet*

*And, if you missed where it all started,*
*check out*
*SANTIAGO'S CONVENIENT FIANCÉE*
*by Annie O'Neil*
*ALEJANDRO'S SEXY SECRET*
*by Amy Ruttan*
*RAFAEL'S ONE NIGHT BOMBSHELL*
*by Tina Beckett*

*All available now!*

# MILLS & BOON®
## Large Print Medical

## September

| | |
|---|---|
| **Their Secret Royal Baby** | Carol Marinelli |
| **Her Hot Highland Doc** | Annie O'Neil |
| **His Pregnant Royal Bride** | Amy Ruttan |
| **Baby Surprise for the Doctor Prince** | Robin Gianna |
| **Resisting Her Army Doc Rival** | Sue MacKay |
| **A Month to Marry the Midwife** | Fiona McArthur |

## October

| | |
|---|---|
| **Their One Night Baby** | Carol Marinelli |
| **Forbidden to the Playboy Surgeon** | Fiona Lowe |
| **A Mother to Make a Family** | Emily Forbes |
| **The Nurse's Baby Secret** | Janice Lynn |
| **The Boss Who Stole Her Heart** | Jennifer Taylor |
| **Reunited by Their Pregnancy Surprise** | Louisa Heaton |

## November

| | |
|---|---|
| **Mummy, Nurse...Duchess?** | Kate Hardy |
| **Falling for the Foster Mum** | Karin Baine |
| **The Doctor and the Princess** | Scarlet Wilson |
| **Miracle for the Neurosurgeon** | Lynne Marshall |
| **English Rose for the Sicilian Doc** | Annie Claydon |
| **Engaged to the Doctor Sheikh** | Meredith Webber |